One look and he knew he was in deep trouble.

"Jack Sanders?"

"In the flesh." He met Kelly's gaze and then looked away quickly.

"What are you doing here?"

"I'm with Prescott Personal Securities." He didn't want her to get the wrong idea—whatever that may be.

"Oh." She stepped aside, and he entered the spacious suite, taking in everything at once the way he'd been trained to do—but still taking in too much of Kelly.

There had been plenty of women since Kelly, beautiful and sexy women. He'd liked them just fine. It was only that the timing had never been right for making any of the relationships permanent.

He halted his runaway thoughts. No way he was going there. He never took chances with client's lives, and he damn sure wouldn't start with Kelly's.

JOANNA WAYNE

24/7

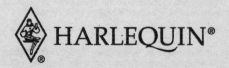

HARLEQUIN®

TORONTO • NEW YORK • LONDON
AMSTERDAM • PARIS • SYDNEY • HAMBURG
STOCKHOLM • ATHENS • TOKYO • MILAN • MADRID
PRAGUE • WARSAW • BUDAPEST • AUCKLAND

A special thanks to Allison Lyons and Sean Mackiewicz for creating the wonderful world of Prescott Personal Securities. And a big smile for all the authors involved in this series, a great team who made working on the book both satisfying and fun. And a wish of magic to lovers everywhere.

Special thanks and acknowledgment are given to Joanna Wayne for her contribution to the BODYGUARDS UNLIMITED, DENVER, CO miniseries.

ISBN-13: 978-0-373-69242-2
ISBN-10: 0-373-69242-0

24/7

ABOUT THE AUTHOR

Joanna was born and raised in Shreveport, Louisiana, and received her undergraduate and graduate degrees from LSU-Shreveport. She moved to New Orleans in 1984 and found the mix of cultures, music, history, food and sultry Southern classics along with her love of reading a natural impetus for beginning her writing career.

Now, dozens of published books later, Joanna has made a name for herself as being on the cutting edge of romantic suspense in both series and single-title novels. She has been on the Waldens Bestselling List for romance and has won many industry awards. She is a popular speaker at writing organizations and local community functions and has taught creative writing at the University of New Orleans Metropolitan College.

She currently resides in a small community forty miles north of Houston, Texas, with her husband. Though she still has many family and emotional ties to Louisiana, she loves living in the Lone Star state. You may write Joanna at P.O. Box 265, Montgomery, Texas 77356.

Books by Joanna Wayne

HARLEQUIN INTRIGUE

CAST OF CHARACTERS

Jack Sanders—Prescott Personal Securities (PPS) agent hired to protect Kelly Warner and her daughter, Alexandra.

Kelly Warner—Wife to Nick Warner; a woman whom it seems everyone is out to kill.

Nick Warner—Actor with lots of secrets, some deadly.

Alexandra Warner—Four-year-old daughter of Nick and Kelly Warner.

Mitchell Caruthers—Nick Warner's manager/publicist.

Hal Hayden—Nick Warner's "friend."

Detective Gilly Carter—Denver detective investigating Nick's murder.

Drake Patton—Actor friend of Kelly Warner.

Devon Degrazzia and Billy Sheffield—Part of the local criminal element.

Karen Butte—Investigative reporter with lots to lose.

Evangeline Prescott—Owner and hands-on manager of PPS.

William "Lenny" Leonard—PPS technical support man, a real whiz at the computer.

Sara Montgomery & Cameron Morgan—PPS agents.

Angel—Goth-queen receptionist at PPS.

Chapter One

Friday, 3:12 a.m.
Rented house just outside Denver

Kelly woke from a restless sleep and lay in the middle of the king-size bed, alone as usual. Wouldn't the paparazzi love to have a shot of this? The wife of sexy, rugged film star, Nick Warner, stuck in the rambling, rented ranch house with only her four-year-daughter for company while her husband partied without her.

Stretching, she pushed back the sheet and comforter and threw her feet over the side of the bed. The house creaked and groaned as she padded barefoot to the bathroom. Renting the house, a rambling structure on the edge of town, had been her idea.

The glitz and glamour surrounding premiers at the Mile High Film Festival turned Denver hotels into a media circus, and Kelly just plain wasn't up to it. She was about to crawl back into bed when she heard her daughter calling for her daddy.

"I'm coming, sweetheart." She wasn't Daddy, but she'd have to do. She stepped into her slippers and pulled on her robe. The house was downright drafty.

Kelly found her daughter sitting up and clutching her worn Pooh bear.

"I want Daddy."

"He's not back yet. Did you have a bad dream?"

"No, but Daddy's here. I saw him."

Kelly sat on the edge of the bed and pulled Alex into her arms. "No one's here but us."

"Daddy was in the hall," Alex said insistently. "He stopped right outside my room, but he didn't come in."

A thread of apprehension wove its way along Kelly's nerve endings, but she brushed it aside. It couldn't have been Nick. He never returned from a night of partying quietly. And it couldn't be anyone else. The security guard that Nick had hired was just outside.

Kelly tousled Alex's soft blond curls. "Daddy's not home yet, sweetheart. You must have dreamed it. Would you like a glass of milk? That might help you get back to sleep."

"Yes, ma'am."

"I'll get it." Kelly was halfway down the hallway when she sensed movement behind her. Her pulse skyrocketed, and she spun around.

A man wearing a ski mask clamped a meaty hand over her mouth and twisted one arm behind her back. "Keep quiet. You don't want that little girl getting in the middle of this."

Her pulse raced. *Oh, God, don't let him hurt Alex!*

He dropped his hand from her mouth. "Where's your husband?"

"He's asleep in the back bedroom," she lied. "He has a gun, and if he hears any noise, he'll come out here."

"You're lying. I've checked the entire house. He's not here."

"No, but there's a guard outside, and if you don't get out of here right now, I'll scream, and he'll hear me."

"There *was* a guard. Now cut the lying. Where is Nick?"

"He's on his way home from a party. He'll be here any second."

"Where's the party?"

"I don't know. What do you want with him?"

He put his face next to hers, and the sickening stench of sweat and garlic made her gag. "That's between me and him, pretty lady." One hand slipped to her right breast.

"Get your hands off me."

"Looks like you'd be glad to have a real man after living with Nick Warner." He shoved her, sending her crashing against the wall. By the time she steadied herself, he was gone.

Her heart pounded in her chest as she walked to the door, afraid to even imagine what she'd find. The door was open, letting in a blast of cold air. She stepped outside.

The guard was there, lying facedown in a pool of blood.

Friday, 8:58 a.m.
Prescott Personal Securities (PPS) Headquarters

"I'M NOT THE MAN for this job."

"Care to explain that remark?"

No, but Jack Sanders knew he'd have to. Evangeline Prescott was the most accommodating boss he'd ever worked for, but she put a lot of thought into the assignments she handed out at Prescott Personal Securities, and she'd expect valid reasons for any kind of protest.

Jack leaned back in his desk chair, but avoided eye contact. "I know the woman involved."

Evangeline pressed the palms of her hands on the back of his desk and leaned closer. "You know Kelly Warner?"

"Well, I did—years ago. She was Kelly O'Conner back then."

"How well did you know her?"

Barely. Intimately. Both answers were correct. "We went to the same high school our senior year."

"That's all? One year of high school?"

"Pretty much."

"Why do I get the feeling you're leaving out a few pertinent details? Did you date?"

"Not exactly."

"An attraction?"

"You could call it that."

Evangeline dropped to the chair opposite his desk and crossed her legs, swinging her right foot, the way she did when she was thinking hard about something. She had great legs. Actually, she pretty much had great everything for a woman who had to be forty or damned close. Long, curly blond hair that she usually wore pulled up and knotted at the nape of her neck. Piercing blue eyes. Nice body.

But there was no getting the wrong idea with Evangeline. Anytime she was inside the doors of PPS Headquarters, she was all business.

Evangeline glanced down at the sheaf of papers she was holding, then raised her gaze to study Jack. "So you shared an attraction with a soap opera star, and never told us. Such modesty."

"She wasn't a star in high school."

"Actually, she was never much of a star," Evangeline said, "but she is beautiful. I'm guessing she was in high school, as well."

"Yeah." Damned good-looking. And sexy as hell. And… He shook his head to clear the unsettling thoughts.

"You might have a couple of awkward moments with Kelly, but I still think you're the man for the job."

"Why is that?"

"You're a smooth talker. You can hang with the Hollywood types, and you'll look good on the red carpet."

"Red carpet?" He groaned. "Tell me you're kidding."

"Afraid not. Nick Warner wants a bodyguard to accompany his wife and daughter for their entire five-day stay in Denver, and that includes tonight's premiere of his film, *Savage Thunder*."

Jack pushed back from his desk, stood and walked to the huge window on the right side of his cubicle. The view was great from the top of the skyscraper, the city below them, snowcapped mountains in the distance.

And now Kelly O'Conner Warner was here in his city. "Any special reason for a bodyguard?" Jack asked. "Or is Nick Warner just looking for someone to punch out a few paparazzi?"

Evangeline walked over and stood beside him. "Someone broke into the house where they were staying last night. Kelly and her daughter were home alone."

"The guy didn't…"

"No, all he did was push her around," Evangeline said, saving him the pain of voicing his fears.

"Where was Nick while this was going on?"

"Out. That's all I know. Nick Warner's requested protection for his wife and daughter, and I've assured him that we can handle the task. You'll head up the operation, but you can have all the manpower you need."

Jack felt a knot of cold fury settling in his chest as Evangeline explained what she knew about the break-in. He didn't want to think of Kelly at all, but he definitely didn't want to envision her with some stinking punk.

"There's more," Evangeline said.

"Like what?"

"The intruder left a calling card."

Jack stiffened, dreading to hear what might come next.

"Home Security, Inc., had been hired to guard the ranch house during the Warner's stay. The young guard on duty last night was murdered. Kelly found his body."

"Sonofabitch! Which detective covered the guard's murder?"

"Gilly Carter."

"He's better than most."

Evangeline nodded her agreement. "There's still more."

"Hit me with it."

"One of our regular informants reported a rumor that there's a hit out on one of the celebrities attending tonight's film festival. We haven't been able to verify any of that, and his information was very sketchy."

"Who's the snitch?"

"The one they call Blackie."

"He's on again, off again."

"We can't take chances. PPS has several clients attending the major events tonight, so we're heightening all our security details. Now, do you still want to turn down the case?"

Yes, for a hundred reasons, all of them having to do with seeing Kelly again. But he wouldn't, for a hundred more, all of them having to do with the fact that some murderous animal had put his hands on her and that there could be more to come.

He stepped back from the window. "Well if you need a tough, good-looking, smooth-talking guy for the job, I guess it would have to be me." His attempt at nonchalance fell flat even to his own ears. "Where do I report?"

"The Warners have moved from the house to a suite in a downtown hotel." She walked back to the desk and picked up the papers she'd been holding when she walked in. "The information is all here. Can I tell Nick you'll be there within the hour?"

He nodded. "Kelly may request a replacement once she realizes I'm to be her bodyguard."

"If she does, it will be her mistake."

And if she didn't, this might well be his.

Friday, 9:41 a.m.
Denver Hotel Suite

KELLY CHECKED ON Alexandra again, then spread the morning newspaper out in front of her and tried to concentrate on something besides last night's intrusion and the bloody body left at her door.

The hotel suite was lavish and extravagant, the way Nick liked everything in his life to be. The living-dining combination was filled with dark, wooden tables and tailored chairs and couches. Huge bouquets of fresh flowers topped several tables, framed Western prints adorned the walls, and a bowl of fresh fruit and chocolate-covered strawberries sat next to a chilled and very expensive bottle of champagne.

The space opened into two bedrooms, one on each side. Alex was in the bedroom on the right. She was huddled in the middle of one of the double beds watching her favorite TV show. Nick and his manager-publicist-confidant Mitchell Caruthers were sitting on the sofa in the main living area, discussing someone named Mike Lawson, whose story they wanted to option for a movie. And outside the door, two cops were standing guard to make sure that no unauthorized visitor came near the suite.

But there had been a steady stream of guests. A reporter from the local newspaper whom Nick had granted an interview. A camera crew from a TV station. And Hal Hayden, who'd hung around most of the morning.

There was a knock at the door. She peeked out to see who was next in the parade. All she saw was one of the cops and a table of food.

She opened the door and the young police officer stepped inside. "Did someone order room service?"

"I did," Mitchell said.

The cop stood back, and a hotel waiter whom Kelly was certain had already been frisked, pushed the cloth-covered cart inside. "Shall I set this up on the dining table?"

"No," Mitchell said. "How about rolling it in there?" He motioned to the empty bedroom. "I have to make a couple of phone calls while I eat."

The last bit of information was directed to Nick who had started sifting through a half-dozen boxes of shoes he'd apparently had sent over from the nearest Nordstrom store.

Mitchell went with his food, and for the first time since their daybreak discussion, Kelly had a few moments alone with her husband. She picked up the mate of the shoe he was trying on. "We need to talk."

He looked at her as if she'd just asked him to drink poison. "Now?"

"What's wrong with now?"

"The premiere is in a matter of hours, and I don't want to get stressed again. You know I break out in a rash when I get too upset."

She resisted the temptation to throw the shoe at him and handed it to him instead. "You may be able to ignore what happened last night, Nick, but I can't. I'm taking Alex back to my parents' house to stay until this blows over. I've called the airlines. We have reservations on a five-o'clock flight."

Nick's mouth flew open. "You promised you'd go to the premiere. You know how much I need you with me tonight."

"I didn't count on having a man murdered practically under my nose when I made that promise."

"It's not like we haven't had threats before. Everyone in this business gets them."

"It's the first time I've been in a killer's hands or had one mere steps from Alex."

"None of which would have happened if you hadn't insisted on staying on that isolated ranch. I tried to talk you out of it."

"So now this is my fault?"

"I didn't mean that the way it sounded," he said.

"I'm extremely concerned about yours and Alex's safety. I just don't see how running to your parents will help."

"It gets us out of Denver."

"Denver isn't the problem. Protection is, and I've hired a bodyguard service to make certain that both you and Alex are safe."

"You hired a guard last night. He's dead."

"Mitchell says that Prescott Personal Securities is the best in the business. You'll be as well protected as the President of the United States. The studio wants you there tonight, and I promised you'd cooperate."

Nick reached for Kelly's hand and pulled her down to the sofa beside him. "I'd never willingly let anyone hurt either of you. Surely you know that."

"I'm not sure what I know anymore."

"Trust me. You and Alex will be safe."

"Why did that man break into our house last night? What did he want with you?"

"He was just some lunatic stalker who went over the edge. You know I'd tell you if there was more."

Alex padded into the room before Kelly had time to respond.

"Is it time to get dressed for your big party, Daddy?"

Nick picked her up and set her on his lap. "Not quite, sweetheart, but you are going to be the prettiest girl there."

Nick patted Kelly's knee. "Promise me that you'll cancel the flight. I'll make it worthwhile."

But she wasn't making promises, not until she

talked to the bodyguard, and maybe not then. There was another knock at the door.

The next visitor had arrived.

JACK WAS CONFIDENT he'd gathered his resolve by the time he reached the hotel. Sure, it had taken him an eternity to get over one night with Kelly, but he'd been young and gullible. He'd toughened up a lot in the years since then. If nothing else, the army had made a man of him—and put a few pins in his left leg.

There had been plenty of women since Kelly, beautiful and sexy women. He'd liked them just fine. It was only that the timing had never been right for making any of the relationships permanent.

Kelly probably wasn't nearly as terrific as he remembered her. More likely, she was a spoiled Hollywood snob, and he'd feel nothing but relief when this assignment was over.

The cop who'd checked his credentials knocked again, then stepped back as the door opened. And there was Kelly.

One look and he knew he was in deep trouble.

Chapter Two

"Jack Sanders?"

"In the flesh." He met Kelly's gaze and then looked away quickly. The air in the stuffy hall seemed charged with her presence.

"What are you doing here? I mean, how did you know I—"

"I'm with Prescott Personal Securities," he interrupted, before she got the wrong idea—whatever that might be. "Your husband called and requested our services."

"Oh. You're here for that." She stepped aside, and he entered the spacious suite, taking in everything at once the way he'd been trained to do—but still taking in too much of Kelly. Her perfume was light and flowery, her eyes as green as he remembered them, but shadowed instead of sparkling the way they had when they'd—

He halted his runaway thoughts. No way he was going there. "Jack Sanders," he said extending his hand to the man standing behind Kelly. "With Prescott Personal Securities."

"Yeah, I heard. I'm Nick Warner." The guy moved his gaze from Jack to Kelly. "Do you two know each other?"

"We went to the same high school, at least for our senior year," Kelly said.

Nick gave Jack a quick once-over, then frowned as if he'd come out lacking. "So you're from around Lake Tahoe?"

"No. I'm from Montana," Jack said. "I lived in the Lake Tahoe area for a year."

Jack had made it a point never to see one of Nick's films, but he'd caught him a few times on late-night television shows. Nick was actually larger in the flesh, an inch or so taller than Jack's six feet two inches, with broad shoulders and muscular biceps. His muscles flexed beneath the white T-shirt he was wearing, and Jack wondered if he were half as tough as the image he tried to project.

Nick put a possessive arm around Kelly's shoulders. "It's nice that you and Kelly already know each other. That might make this a little easier on her. She had a rough night. I guess your supervisor filled you in on that."

"Some. I'll want to hear it from Kelly, as well." The door behind Nick was open and Jack could hear a TV playing in the other room. "How large is the suite?"

"This room," Nick said, motioning to the living-dining area where they were standing, "and two bedrooms."

"So that would be three doors that open into the hall?"

"Yes, but I already have a police detail working that. Your responsibility will only be Kelly and our daughter, Alex. I'll expect you to accompany them wherever they want to go including the premiere tonight. But keep a low profile at the premiere. We don't want to draw any attention to you."

His authoritative tone ticked Nick off, not that he wasn't used to it. A lot of the celebrities who hired PPS started out thinking they gave the orders. "I'm afraid it doesn't work like that with PPS, Mr. Warner. If someone's under my protection, I can't guarantee a low profile."

"I've already checked, and the security at the venue is more than adequate. I expect you to…"

Nick stopped midsentence, evidently changing his mind about the ultimatum he seemed about to issue. "Do what's necessary," he said. "And don't worry about the cost. Nothing is more important to me than my wife's and daughter's safety."

"Then we need to start with the facts about what happened last night and what led up to it."

There was a knock at the door. Jack watched as Nick left Kelly's side to greet Karen Butte, a local who did investigative reporting for one of the national news networks as well as one of the local channels. He'd met her last year when she'd been investigating a suspected terrorist cell in the Denver area. It was a cell that he'd successfully infiltrated and fortunately had stopped them before they'd carried out a bombing plot.

She and Jack exchanged hellos, but her demeanor was all business. He wondered what she was investigating that she'd need to talk to Nick about.

Another man stepped out of one of the bedrooms. He appeared to be in his midthirties, around six feet tall, short brown hair, neatly dressed in tailored gray slacks and a light blue dress shirt.

"Mitchell, could you meet with Jack Sanders and Kelly in the empty bedroom while I give Miss Butte a short interview?" Nick said. "Jack's the bodyguard I hired for Kelly. Give him your full cooperation and sign whatever he needs signed."

Mitchell smiled. "Absolutely." He turned to Jack and offered his hand and a limp handshake. "Mitchell Caruthers."

Jack followed Kelly and Mitchell into the bedroom. He wasn't sure what Nick meant by full cooperation, but he had an idea that it wasn't the same as his. It didn't matter. They'd do this Jack's way—or they wouldn't do it at all. He never took chances with clients' lives, and he damn sure wouldn't start with Kelly's.

KELLY WORKED to get her reactions under control. Her nerves were already rattled, and having Jack

Sanders show up at her door did nothing to settle them. She smoothed her hair and wished she'd put on makeup. Not that it mattered. She and Jack were ancient history. Still, it was nice—and a little sur- prising—that he remembered her.

Mitchell motioned for Jack to take a seat in the room. Jack moved toward a chair but stood until Kelly settled on the tweed love seat. Mitchell grabbed a pad of paper from his desk and took a seat beside her.

"Your firm comes highly recommended," Mitchell said. Nick had me check that out before he contacted you. But before we sign any official agreement, I'd like to know your personal credentials for the job."

"A fair question." Jack sat back and crossed his right foot over his left knee. "I was in the army for eleven years, seven of those in a special combat unit trained for search-and-rescue operations and infil- trating terrorist camps."

"Why did you leave the army?"

"I was injured while on an undercover operation in Afghanistan."

"So the army dropped you when you could no longer adequately perform your duties?"

"No, I left the army because I was ready for new challenges."

"But you are disabled?"

"No. I'm fully recovered and extremely able. That's why I'm here."

Mitchell's cell phone rang. He checked the ID.

"Personal," he said. "You'll have to excuse me a minute." He took the call as he walked into the bathroom, closing the door behind him and leaving Kelly and Jack alone.

Awareness trickled along Kelly's nerve endings, and she felt the heat rise to her cheeks. Fortunately, Jack didn't seem to notice.

"I'd like to hear your version of what happened last night."

She took a few seconds to pull the fractured, frightening facts from her memory and get them in order. "It was somewhere around 3:00 a.m. My daughter woke up and I was getting her a glass of milk when all of a sudden this man grabbed me from behind."

"Was anyone staying in the house besides you and your daughter?"

"My husband, Nick, but he wasn't there. He was…" She hesitated. There was nowhere to go with the statement, at least nowhere she wanted to go with Jack. "My husband was busy with social activities related to the premiere of his movie."

"So you and your daughter were alone?"

"Nick had hired a security service to watch the house. There was no reason to think we wouldn't be perfectly safe."

Jack nodded, and she went on with her story, repeating it exactly as it happened, right down to finding the bloody body at her door.

"Did the intruder threaten you or your daughter at any time during the confrontation?"

"Yes."

"What did he threaten?"

She tried, but couldn't remember exactly what he'd said. She'd felt threatened, feared for Alex, thought the man might rape her. Yet…

"The threat wasn't detailed," she admitted, "but the intruder led me to believe he might hurt Alex if I screamed or caused any kind of commotion."

"But he didn't put that into words?"

Kelly shook her head. "Not exactly. He said I should keep Alex out of it, or something to that effect. I took that to mean I shouldn't alarm her so that she came into the hallway where the man was holding me."

"What about you, Kelly?"

"What about me?"

"I know the man frightened you and knocked you down, but did he give any specific threats about harming you?"

Finally she saw where Jack was going with this. "It was my husband he wanted, but he killed a guard. He might just as easily have killed Alex or me."

Jack leaned forward. "I'm not trying to belittle the danger. I'm just trying to understand it. The better handle we have on what this man is after, the easier it is to intercept him."

Finally, she met Jack's gaze. His eyes crinkled at the corners—pulled by tiny wrinkles that hadn't been there fourteen years ago. But he still had that indefinable something that had driven her half-crazy back then.

"Did he say what he wanted with Nick?"

"No. My husband thinks he's a stalker who went over the edge."

"Did he appear to be drunk or on drugs?"

"Not that I could tell. I didn't smell alcohol on his breath. He did smell of garlic and sweat, though."

"What else did you notice about him?"

"His hands were rough. When he touched my breast—"

"Whoa!" Jack said, breaking into her explanation. "I was told he didn't violate you in any way."

"He just skimmed my breast with his hand. That was all. When I complained he knocked me against the wall and left."

Jack's expression hardened, as if the man's touching her changed things. "Can you describe his physical appearance?"

"It was dark, so I couldn't see a lot of details, but he was medium build, taller than me by a few inches, but not as tall as Nick—or you. Oh, yeah, and he had a tattoo on his arm. The light was too dim to make out the design."

"Did he wear any kind of mask or covering over his face?"

"A ski mask. I told all of this to Gilly Carter. He's the detective who showed up after the original patrolman answered my 911 call."

"Did you get any sense that you might have met him before?"

"No, but there are always so many people hanging

around Nick that I could have met him and still not recognized his voice. Next time I'll be much more observant."

Next time. The thought sent a chill through her.

Jack raised his right arm to scratch a spot just behind his ear, and she glimpsed the shoulder holster beneath his denim jacket. She wasn't surprised that he was wearing a weapon, but his protector status made her even more aware of how much he'd changed from their high school days.

"Have you been to one of your husband's premieres before? Jack asked.

"Several times."

"Then what's the big deal about going to this one instead of staying out of crowds for a few days? Aren't they all pretty much the same?"

"To an outsider perhaps, but not to the star."

"And that would be your husband?"

"Exactly. Alex and I came to Denver specifically for the premiere. I'm having second thoughts about it after last night, but I guess there's no real reason not to go."

"How do you figure?"

"The intruder obviously didn't want to harm either Alex or me. If he had, he would have done it."

"The man who broke into your house is a killer. You can't be too careful as long as a lunatic like that is on the loose. If my questions made you think otherwise, I'm sorry I misled you."

"Then you don't think our attending the premiere is a good idea?"

"Give me some time to check it out. I have some men from PPS evaluating the security at the theater. We have lots of extra protection we can put in place, but if I feel there's any risk at all, my recommendation will be that you forgo the event."

"And catch the next plane back to L.A.?"

"That's your call. What about this Mitchell guy?" Jack asked. "What's his official job around here?"

"Mitchell Caruthers is Nick's manager, publicist, and sometimes voice of reason."

"Do you trust him?"

"Totally. He's been with Nick since his first major movie. He makes most of the business decisions. Mitchell has an excellent head for business whereas Nick is the social animal." And that was putting it mildly.

Kelly looked up as the door opened. It was Nick, and looking none too happy. Evidently the interview had not gone well—which would explain why it had ended so quickly.

"Sorry I had to leave you two alone," he said, dropping to the love seat beside Kelly. "High school chums, huh? Small world."

"It can be," Jack said.

"So have you convinced my pretty wife here that it's perfectly safe for her and our adorable daughter to go to the premiere tonight?" His tone was much edgier than the words warranted.

"I haven't come to that conclusion yet myself," Jack said.

"The whole purpose of hiring you is to insure their safety so that they can attend."

"I understand that."

"So can you do it or not?"

"I can keep them safe, but that might require scrapping the big event."

"I see. So when do you expect to make a definitive decision on that?"

"Within an hour or two."

"I guess we have no choice but to wait until then. You can let yourself out—Jack, isn't it."

"I could, if I were leaving."

"You don't have a lot of time to waste sitting around here renewing old times with Kelly."

Jack stood as if on cue. "I won't be sitting or chatting. I'll be conducting the groundwork to insure your wife and daughter's safety from this suite."

"I expected you to only be with her when she leaves the hotel."

"You hired full protection for Kelly and Alex, and that means I'll be wherever Kelly and Alex are—or very close—24/7."

"I see. Well if you don't mind, I'd like a word alone with my wife. Your 24/7 does allow for that, doesn't it?"

"Sure thing. Marriage pulls rank, as long as I don't consider it a risk." He smiled, as if that were a private joke the two of them shared. But if anything the tension in the room grew thicker.

Twenty-four/seven. Her and Jack, and memories

of the wildest night of her life. That might not be the best of ideas. But if it took this to insure Alex's safety, she'd just have to handle it.

Friday, 6:55 p.m.
Nick Warner's hotel suite

NICK AND HIS ENTOURAGE had left for the theater thirty minutes ago, leaving Jack to wait for the two Warner females, who were still in their bedroom getting ready. He was wearing a rented tux he'd had delivered to the hotel. A good bodyguard fit in with his surroundings.

Nick hadn't liked Jack's final decision, but he'd gone along with it. Kelly and Alex would attend the premiere and watch the film from the seats right next to Nick, but there would be no red-carpet arrival.

Security inside the theater was top-notch as reported, but there was no way to fully protect anyone in the hordes of spectators crowding around the entrance. So Jack would escort Kelly and Alex through a back door guarded by a PPS agent. He'd walk them to their seats and then he'd take the one on the aisle right behind Kelly and Alexandra, where he could keep his eye on them every second. They'd make their getaway the second the credits started to roll.

The door to the bedroom opened and Alex danced out, twirling so that she looked like a frothy, spinning top. "Do you like my dress?"

"Wow! You look like a princess."

"Like Cinderella?"

"Much prettier than Cinderella."

"But I don't have glass slippers."

"No, but you have pretty red ones."

"They're shiny, too."

"Very shiny."

Alex jumped to the sofa, settling in the white swirl of her skirts. She poked her little legs straight out and gave her shiny shoes a quick brush with her fingertips. "Are you Daddy's friend or Mommy's friend?"

"Can't I be both?"

"Well, my daddy's friends mostly talk to him, 'cause they're movie stars. My daddy is, too. He's very famous."

"I've heard that."

"Are you a movie star?"

"No."

"Then I guess you're Mommy's friend."

Nice the way four-year-olds categorized things so simply. Either the round hole or the square one and no indistinguishable shapes that didn't fit. He was pretty sure the relationship he'd had with Kelly wouldn't meet Dr. Phil's criteria for friendship.

The rustle of silk caught his attention. He turned and felt a slow burn deep in his gut. This was not the vivacious high school beauty who'd sent his world spinning fourteen years ago. She was a fully developed knockout.

"Sorry to be so long. My parents just heard about last night's break-in on the news. I had to assure them a dozen times that Alex and I are fine. I thought it best not to tell my dad you were our bodyguard, however."

"Yeah." It was all he could manage with his throat feeling as if he'd swallowed an avocado whole.

"Better go to the bathroom before we leave, Alex," she said.

Alex jumped from the sofa and planted her hands on her tiny hips. "I don't need to."

"Go anyway. It's easier here than at the theater."

Alex puckered her lips as if she thought going to the bathroom on demand was a ridiculous idea, but she skipped away, leaving Jack alone with Kelly.

"You look nice," she said.

"This old thing?" He tried to make light of the moment, though the feelings coursing through him were anything but. "You, too," he said, uttering the biggest understatement of his life.

The long green gown hugged her magnificent body, then widened to an enticing swirl around her ankles. The bodice plunged to reveal seductive cleavage and emphasize her perfect breasts. He took a deep breath and exhaled slowly, determined to keep things in perspective.

Alex skipped back into the room. "Now can we go?"

"As soon as Mr. Sanders gives the word."

"Let's do it," he said. He opened the door and gave the area a quick once-over. Nick's paid police patrol had been supplemented by one very efficient PPS employee.

"The elevator won't stop until you reach the lobby," Paul said. "The car's waiting at the side entrance. Sara Montgomery's driving the escort car tonight."

Sara was one of PPS's top agents. She looked like a model and handled a gun like a sharpshooter. And she could spot trouble faster than crows could find roadkill. He was glad to have her on his team.

"Is PPS always this overpowering?" Kelly asked.

"We do what we think is necessary. The break-in and murder last night necessitates a higher level of security. Fortunately, your husband gave us the go-ahead to do whatever was needed."

Jack took Kelly's elbow and Alex grabbed Jack's hand, pushing her small palm against his much larger one. He was all about protection now.

Friday, 7:40 p.m.
Mile High Theater for the Arts

THE MAN WATCHED from a distance as Nick Warner acted the role of devoted husband and loving father. He was riding a high, thinking that nothing could shake his world. But the bigger they were the harder they fell.

Nick and his beautiful wife, Kelly, would both be going down.

Chapter Three

Friday, 10:08 p.m.
Mile High Theater of the Arts

Jack stood as the credits started to roll, reaching forward and tapping Kelly on the shoulder as he did, their prearranged signal that it was time to leave the theater.

She jumped to her feet and tugged Alex from her chair. "Time to go, sweetie," she whispered.

"I want to stay with Daddy."

"We'll see him later."

"You don't have to leave so quickly," Nick said, standing himself now and swooping Alex into his arms. "It's safe in here. Smile and act happy."

Jack tensed. He didn't need this. Their chance to sneak out early was disappearing fast as others started to stand and gather their coats. He put his mouth to Nick's ear. "Put Alex down. Now!"

"Or what?" he mocked. "You'll shoot me?"

It was damned tempting. The lights went up, unleashing a flurry of activity. A rush of people hurried to congratulate Nick, who had pushed past Kelly and into the center aisle. A tall blond guy with a booming voice led the cheering cavalry and blocked the escape route.

"Magnificent," he crowed, while others shouted their compliments.

"You're the man!"

"A sure winner. You've never looked better."

"Superb acting."

Basking in his glory, Nick let Alex slide from his arms. Jack shoved his way into the aisle, picked up Alex, and then crawled over a row of seats to get to Kelly. He nudged her toward the center of the row, a safer situation than trying to propel them through the mass of bodies crowding around Nick.

Jack studied the crowd. "Stay right with me," he instructed as he moved toward the left aisle. In theory, Nick was right that there should be nothing to worry about inside the theater. Everyone entering the building had been through a metal detector and a bag check. The only armed people inside should be him, other PPS employees there with their celebrity clients, and the regular theater security. Still, this was a change in plans, and Jack didn't like deviations.

Finally, he saw the break they needed and herded Kelly toward a side exit. He called in the change to Sara just as he spotted a man in a tuxedo rushing toward them. The guy looked familiar, but Jack couldn't place him.

"Stop right there," Jack said, his hand resting on the butt of his gun.

The man's brows shot up. "Do you know who I am?"

"Can't say that I do."

"It's okay, Jack. He's a friend."

"What's going on?" the friend asked.

"Nothing," Kelly answered. "I just want to get Alex out of the crowd. Call me later."

"Why don't I drive you and Alex back to the hotel?"

"Thanks, but we have a ride."

"With him?" He nodded toward Jack.

"Yes. I'll explain later, Drake. Right now I just need to get out of here."

Drake. The name triggered recall. No wonder the guy looked familiar. He was Drake Patton, one of the hottest of the hot, even giving Johnny Depp and Brad Pitt a run for the box office money. Jack disliked him instantly, but he refused to let himself think about why. He had to stay focused on the task at hand, and the task was getting Kelly and Alex to total safety.

He hurried them toward the door, almost making it before a middle-aged woman dripping with diamonds latched onto Kelly's arm.

"Nick was fantastic. You must be so proud of him."

"Yes, I have to go, Olivia."

"But you must come to my party. It's in Nick's

honor. I've invited the whole cast and everyone who's anyone."

"I have to take Alex back to the hotel."

Kelly was insistent, but the woman seemed to be looking right past her. The blank stare made Jack nervous. He pried the woman's hand from Kelly's arm.

"Sorry, Olivia," he said, "but we do have to go."

Sara was just outside, parked beneath the overhang, the engine of the PPS escort car running. Jack didn't breathe easy until both his charges were inside and the car was speeding away from the venue.

"Where's Daddy?" Alex asked.

"Daddy had to stay at the theater for a while so he could talk to the people who came to see him in the movie."

He stayed because he was a royal jerk rushing off to party with a bunch of publicity seekers when any normal, red-blooded man in the place would have been glad to go home with Kelly.

Even Drake Patton. No, especially Drake Patton. The way he'd looked at Kelly yelled lust—and more. The guy had a thing for her. She might have a thing for him, as well.

Not that Jack cared. Why should he? Kelly was just a job. A blast from the past that he was totally over.

"Thanks, Jack," she whispered.

He turned and let their gazes meet. "Just doing my job."

She took his hand and squeezed it. "You do it well."

Totally over her, and that unexpected burning in

his chest was from the extra jalapeños he'd put on his burger back at the hotel.

Saturday, 2:19 a.m.
Warner's hotel suite

KELLY WOKE AND SAT UP in bed quickly, thoughts of the previous night making her blood run cold. But tonight all was quiet. Moonlight gleamed through the soft white curtain at the window, painting the silent room in silvery streaks.

She scooted from her bed and tiptoed to the other one to check on Alex. She was sound asleep, her cheek resting against the plush belly of her Pooh bear. Kelly kissed her softly on the cheek then went back to her own bed, though she was wide-awake now.

A line of dim light stared at her from beneath the door, reminding her that Jack Sanders was only a few steps away. She'd offered to have a roll-away bed sent up for him, but he'd assured her that he preferred the couch. She pictured him there now, wrapped in an extra sheet the housekeeping staff had brought up for him, his head resting on one of the hotel pillows.

Jack, the protector. Most definitely *not* the same old Jack.

Fourteen years ago, he'd been the danger. He rode his Harley way too fast, drank beer long before he was legal, had a tattoo on his right forearm. Surely that was still there.

Kelly's minister father had seen him as a troublemaker who was bound to wind up in prison before he was thirty. He'd grounded Kelly for two weeks when he'd smelled whiskey on her breath and she'd guiltily confessed to having sipped from Jack's flask when she and her friends had run into him at the lake.

She'd missed her senior prom because of that, and the beautiful blue dress she and her mother had bought in Sacramento on Kelly's eighteenth birthday had been returned unworn. Prom night had started as the worst in Kelly's life.

It had ended in her sneaking out of the house and losing her virginity to the dangerous and incredibly sexy Jack Sanders. It was the last time she'd seen him—until now.

She crawled back into bed and closed her eyes, then opened them to the shrill ring of the hotel phone. She dived for it before it woke Alex. It wasn't until she heard Jack's voice on the line that she remembered his rule that she was to let him screen all calls. She didn't speak, but kept the receiver to her ear.

"This is the University of Colorado Hospital. I'm calling for Mrs. Nick Warner."

"I'm Mrs. Warner," she blurted out. "What's wrong?"

"Your husband was brought to the hospital a few minutes ago by ambulance."

"What happened?"

"He was shot twice in the stomach. He's lost a lot of blood and is experiencing other complications. The doctors are trying to stabilize him for surgery."

"Is he conscious?"

"Yes, and asking for you. I'd advise you to come as quickly as you can."

"He's going to make it, isn't he?"

"He's critical. The doctor will see you and explain more when you get here. Your husband's in the Intensive Care Unit. Take the elevator to the third floor and stop at the nurses' station to your right."

"Where is the hospital?"

"I know where it is," Jack said.

Crazy, but she'd forgotten he was on the line. She hung up the phone and started unbuttoning her pajama top with trembling fingers. Nick, shot twice in the stomach. The shooter had to be the same man who'd broken into their rented house last night.

Nick had made sure she and Alex were safe, but apparently he hadn't been nearly that protective of himself. That was like him to take partying more seriously than precautions. But then the way he celebrated life was the first thing that had attracted her to him.

There was a soft rap at the bedroom door just as she'd shed her top. "Come in," she murmured, reaching for the lavender sweatshirt she'd changed into after the premiere.

"Do you want Sara to stay with Alex or do you want to take her to the hospital with us?"

With us? Twenty-four/seven. Of course he'd be going with her, though now that the shooter had found his real victim, he was probably on the run. "Who's Sara?"

"Our chauffeur to and from the premiere. She's one of our agents."

"She's a PPS agent? But she's so pretty."

"She's top-notch."

Kelly hated the thought of leaving Alex with anyone, but she didn't want to wake her and drag her to the hospital, either, especially when she wasn't sure exactly what she'd find when she got there.

"Are you certain she'll be okay with Sara?"

"Totally safe. Plus if Alex wakes up before we get back, she'll recognize Sara. Alex asked her a ton of questions on the way back from the theater."

Sara and Alex had bonded. And this way Alex would get a full night's sleep. "How long would it take her to get here?"

"Under five minutes. She took a room in the hotel, planned to relieve one of the other agents on duty here at 3:00 a.m., but we can bring someone else in for that."

"Get her," she said, making the only decision that made sense.

He stepped back into the living area and closed the door behind him.

Kelly shivered from a chill that had settled deep in her bones. This was supposed to have been Nick's crowning moment. Now he was fighting for his life.

Fate was a master of cruel deceptions.

Saturday, 2:56 a.m.
University of Colorado Hospital

KELLY STEPPED INTO the curtain-enclosed cubicle to find Nick lying strapped to a narrow bed, his face pasty-white, his eyes closed. The numerous tubes and wires attached to his body shocked her at first, and she clasped the canvaslike fabric of the curtain in her shaky fingers.

A nurse stepped to her side. "Are you Kelly?"

"Yes. Kelly Warner. I'm the patient's wife."

"Your husband was calling for you when they first brought him in. You and someone named Mitchell. Thankfully, he's quieted now."

Kelly walked to the edge of the bed and placed her hand on one of his. His eyes remained closed. "Should I say something to him or let him rest?"

"You can try talking to him. I'm not sure if he'll hear you or respond."

Kelly leaned in close. "I'm here, Nick."

His body jerked and the muscles around his eyes twitched as if he were trying to open them.

"It's okay, Nick. I'll be right here. The doctors are taking good care of you." This time there was no response. She turned to the nurse. "Is he in pain?"

"No. He's heavily medicated. The twitches are reflexive movements."

The bleached white hospital gown covered Nick's legs and private parts, but not the bloodstained bandages wrapped around him from his abdomen to his ribs. "How extensive are his injuries?"

"Dr. Riuski will explain that."

"Is he a surgeon?"

"No. He's an internist and the senior E.R. doctor on the night shift. He's called in a surgeon and a cardiologist, though, and they're both on their way to the hospital. I'll let Dr. Riuski know you've arrived."

The nurse glanced toward Jack, who was standing a few feet behind Kelly. "Visitors are restricted to family."

"Jack is family," she lied, not wanting to get into a lengthy explanation of the situation.

The nurse nodded. "I'll be right back."

Kelly listened to the heavy wheezing from Nick's chest, traced the drawn lines in his face with her gaze, listened to the rhythmic click of the heart monitor as erratic crests and dips passed across the screen.

"Noooo. The gun."

Kelly squeezed Nick's hand. "It's okay. You're in the hospital. You're safe." She wasn't sure he heard her. He seemed to be out of his head.

"Damn list. Nooo. Nooo."

Kelly leaned close to Nick's ear. "You can tell me, Nick. I'm right here."

"Noooo. T…C…M. Noooo."

The muttering dissolved into groans. Kelly stepped back from the bed. "Why would someone do that to him?"

"There are lots of crazy people in the world,"

Jack whispered. "They don't need logical reasons for what they do."

Nick jerked again, and frustration balled in her chest. "Where is that damn doctor? Why aren't they doing anything?"

"I'm right here, Mrs. Warner, and we're doing all we can."

She turned at the voice and saw a young, lanky man in rimless glasses and white lab coat standing just behind Jack. He looked drawn, as if he'd dealt with one too many emergencies tonight. Or as if he dreaded talking to her.

"I'm Kelly Warner," she explained, "Nick's wife."

He nodded. "I'm Dr. Riuski. Why don't we step outside the area?"

She followed him out of the ICU and into a hallway that was pungent with the stringent odors of antiseptics and bleach from the solution a janitor was using to clean the gray floor tiles.

A microphone over her head blared. "Paging Dr. Alvarez." A nurse hurried by with a wheeled tray of implements. Two burly orderlies wheeled a gurney in their direction.

"There's a small conference room just down the hall," Dr. Riuski said. "We can talk better there."

Unlike the nurse, the doctor didn't question Jack's presence. They took a right at the nurses' station and walked a few yards before the doctor stopped and ushered them into a room that appeared more like a makeshift staff lounge than a conference room.

There were cabinets, a counter and a small rectangular table surrounded by six metal folding chairs. A pot of coffee rested on a two-station brewing machine next to an opened package of cookies.

"Would you like coffee?" the doctor asked.

"No thanks," Kelly said, afraid her stomach would reject anything in its shaky condition.

"I'll take a cup," Jack said.

"I'll join you," Dr. Riuski said, pulling two foam cups from a wall-mounted dispenser. He poured a cup for both of them. There was a jar of creamer and a mixed collection of sweeteners, but both men took theirs straight.

Dr. Riuski sat down opposite Kelly and wasted no time getting to the meat of the matter. "It appears that your husband took three bullets. One lodged in the fatty tissue just below his left rib cage. Unfortunately, the other two penetrated his abdomen, tearing through muscle, tissue and countless blood vessels along the way. There's significant internal bleeding and damage to several internal organs, though the urinalysis did not show blood in the urine, at least not yet."

"Can't you operate and remove the bullets?"

"We could, but with his vital signs as unstable as they are now, he'd never survive the surgery. His blood pressure is not only in the danger zone, but he's suffered a mild heart attack."

"I don't understand. You said the bullets lodged in the stomach. Why would he have a heart attack?"

"Your husband had dangerous levels of amphet-amines in his system when he was admitted to the hospital. Even without the bullets, he might have had the heart attack or other organ shutdowns."

"Nick doesn't do drugs."

"I can only tell you what the tests showed."

Kelly waited, expecting some word of optimism from the doctor whose voice suddenly sounded as tired as he looked. It didn't come, and she felt as if icicles were puncturing her nerve endings. She had lots of issues with Nick, but she'd never wanted to see him dead.

"Does he have a chance?"

"I'd say no more than twenty percent, but if he makes it through the night, that could go up."

Eighty percent chance that Alex would never see her father again. Maybe Kelly had been wrong to leave her at the hotel, but Kelly didn't want Alex's last memories of Nick to be of him the way he looked right now. She should remember him laugh-ing, telling her stories, showing her off to all his friends.

The doctor finished his coffee and stood. "I'm sorry I can't be more encouraging, but I feel it's always best to level with the family."

"I appreciate that." But her legs were shaky when she stood, and she stumbled backward. Jack steadied her with a hand on her arm.

"Are you okay?"

"Not really."

"I can give you something to steady your nerves," the doctor offered.

"No, thanks. I'd like to keep a clear head."

She was aware of Jack's hand at the small of her back as she started back toward the ICU. Not quite friend; disturbingly more than a stranger.

They were almost back to Nick's room when a uniformed policeman caught up with them.

"Mrs. Warner?"

"Yes."

"Officer Rick Manning." He flashed an ID. "I'm sorry about your husband. I know this isn't the best time, but I need to ask you a few questions."

She nodded, though she doubted she had the answers he was looking for.

"Who was your husband with tonight?"

"He was going out with some of his friends who were in town for the film festival."

"I need their names."

"I'm sorry. I don't have that information."

"He was shot on a side street in the Larimer Square area. Do you know if he'd been in one of the clubs there?"

"No. I really don't know anything about what happened tonight, and I think I should probably be with my husband in case he regains consciousness."

Jack stepped forward, insinuating himself between her and the officer. "You must have witnesses who can give you this information."

"Not at this point."

"Who reported the shooting?"

"A man who was walking to his car." The officer pulled a pad and pen from his shirt pocket. "Can I have your name and relation to the victim?"

"Jack Sanders, of Prescott Personal Services. I was hired by Nick Warner this morning to protect his wife and daughter."

"But not to protect him?"

"If he'd hired PPS to protect himself, he wouldn't have been shot. You need to notify Detective Gilly Carter and let him know about the shooting so that he can make sure his crime scene is intact."

"No offense, Mr. Sanders, but if the department needs PPS help in handling the investigation, we'll let you know."

"Fine. In the meantime, notify Gilly Carter. And you can go now. Mrs. Warner is not available for questioning at this time unless you have a warrant."

Jack led her back to the ICU. When she stepped inside the unit, she was hit again with the foreign smells and sights and the cold feel of dread.

Tears started to roll down her cheeks.

Jack handed her a tissue. "Don't give up, Kelly. The two of you will have years ahead of you."

But the tears wouldn't stop. The fear and the dread—and the truth—were exploding inside her. She had to confess their twisted marriage to someone. Jack shouldn't be that person. But he was here, and right now, she ached to hold on to someone not even remotely connected to the lies.

Jack put an arm around her shoulder and she leaned her sobbing body against his broad shoulder. "Take me out of here, Jack. Please. I need to talk."

Chapter Four

Jack had never felt more inadequate than he did at this minute. Give him a life to protect, a killer to go up against. Just don't give him Kelly O'Conner with tears in her eyes and her emotions hanging right out there on the sleeve of her delectably soft lavender sweatshirt.

Only she wasn't Kelly O'Conner. She was Kelly Warner, and her emotions were all about her husband. Jack was just the only warm body around who wasn't involved in the serious task of saving Nick's life.

He scanned the waiting room for anyone who looked as if they didn't belong there, his protective instincts on target even if the rest of his brain was skidding into dangerous territory.

Kelly dropped into a plaid armchair and pulled her feet into the seat with her. "I need to explain something."

"Don't explain your tears, Kelly. You're worried about your husband. Any woman would be."

"I am worried about him, but that's not what I need to explain. I can't get through this, not with everyone believing the lies. I can't keep it up. I just can't." Desperation pulled at her voice.

"You're upset."

"I'm very upset. But I'm not Nick's wife. I mean, I am, but just on paper."

Jack had no idea where Kelly was going with this, but he was pretty sure he couldn't handle going there with her right now. Especially not with her talking through sniffles and tears. "This isn't the time to think about that. I'm not the man you should—"

She put up her hand to stop him from interrupting. "Will you please just let me finish this?"

He nodded.

"None of this can go outside this room."

"You have my word on that," he promised, "unless you're about to confess to something illegal."

"No, it's nothing like that."

He hadn't imagined that it would be. More likely it was about an affair she was having with Drake Patton. She probably felt guilty as hell now and wanted to redeem herself. Well, let her, if it eased her conscience. "Is there another man?"

"Oh, not just one. There's been a string of them."

He knew he should have turned down this assignment. "Please, Kelly. Let it go for tonight. You should be telling this to a friend."

"I'm so bottled up. Can't you just please let me talk?"

"Okay. You talk. I'll listen."

"Nick's gay. Our marriage is a sham."

"Nick's the one who's been with lots of other men?"

"Of course. You didn't think it was me?"

"No. No way," he lied.

"I suspected it as long as eighteen months ago, just about the same time the media picked up on it and the rumors started. When I asked him about it, he denied it vehemently."

"Were the two of you still having sex?"

"No, we haven't had sex since right after Alex was born."

"Four years ago?"

"I know it sounds strange, but Nick was on location much of the time, and I got used to satisfying my own needs. Our sex life had never been good anyway, so when he moved to another bedroom, I was relieved. We got along well in other ways. He's fun, loves to party, and he adores Alex. I know it sounds weird, but it seemed enough for a while, especially since I was dealing with my own career going down the tube."

"That will come back."

"No, I wasn't that good, and I've lost the drive for it. But Nick was supportive of me through it all, and that meant a lot to me."

"Then you didn't know he was gay when you married him?"

"No. I'm not even sure he'd fully accepted it himself."

"How long have you known for sure?"

"About six months. I caught him in an extremely compromising position in our pool house. That's when I knew I had to get out of the marriage."

"So you've already filed for divorce?"

"No. By then the rumors of his being gay were cropping up on a regular basis, and the studio was afraid they had contributed to his bad showing at the box office on his last two movies. They'd warned him that if he had one more bomb, they'd drop his contract. He begged me to stay with him until the release of *Savage Thunder*."

"And you agreed?"

"There was no real reason not to. I cared for him and didn't want to see him fail. I just didn't love him. I'm not sorry for any of it. If I'd never married Nick, I wouldn't have Alex. And she's worth any amount of heartbreak. Besides, Nick has his passions and I have mine."

Jack wondered if Drake Patton was one of those passions. He wouldn't ask. It was none of his business. None of this was.

Kelly wiped her eyes again, running the edge of one finger beneath her runny mascara. "I'm sorry. It's just—I'm sorry, that's all."

She stood and started to walk away though the tears were streaming down her face now. Jack didn't really understand what was going on inside her, only that she was hurting. He caught up with her and grabbed her arm, tugging her around to face him.

And then he was the one who lost it. He wrapped his arms around her and pulled her against him as her hot tears and satiny strands of golden hair caressed his neck.

His traitorous body started to harden. God help him, but he wanted Kelly. Wanted her right here in this sterile hospital environment. Wanted her while her gay husband lay nearby fighting for his life.

But he merely held her while she cried.

KELLY CLOSED HER EYES, fighting the tears that burned her eyelids. Weird that it should be Jack Sanders she'd bared her soul to, when she'd never told anyone else. She sniffled and pulled away, turning to see Mitchell Caruthers standing at the door to the waiting room glaring at her and Jack.

"I came as soon as I heard," he said when she met his gaze.

"If Nick wasn't out with you or Hal, who was he with?"

"Nick and Hal were both still at Olivia's party when I went back to the hotel. Hal said he left him in a bar with the drinking still going strong sometime after that. How's Nick?"

"He's critical," she answered. "He's in ICU. They're only letting family in, but you can tell them you're a brother."

"Is he conscious?"

"No."

"Then I guess he hasn't told you who shot him—or why?"

"Unfortunately not. He's just muttered things out of his head."

"What kind of things?"

"A list. A gun. Mostly he just groaned, but the nurse assured me he's not actually in pain." Kelly shared the doctor's explanation with Mitchell. "How did you hear?" she asked.

Mitchell shoved his hands in his pockets, nervously jangling his keys. "Hal Hayden called me at the hotel. He heard about the shooting from his limo driver, who apparently heard it from some cop."

"Who's Hal Hayden?" Jack asked, his first utterance since Mitchell had arrived on the scene.

"He's an actor from *Savage Thunder,* and a friend of Nick's," Mitchell answered, barely glancing at Jack before turning his attention back to Kelly. "It's too bad Nick hasn't said anything rational. Are you sure he didn't mention a name?"

"If he did, I couldn't make it out. I just hope he regains consciousness soon. I was on my way back to stay with him."

Mitchell finally pulled his hands from his pockets and let his jangling keys fall silent. "Do you think I can have a few moments alone with him first? I'd like to say my goodbyes, just in case, even if he doesn't know I'm there."

"Of course, Mitchell. But be prepared. You'll be

shocked when you first see him. He looks…" She hesitated. Nick looked and sounded like a man on the verge of death but she couldn't bring herself to say that. "He's very ill."

She waited until Mitchell walked away before calling her hotel room to check on Alex. Sara answered on the first ring and assured her that everything was fine and that Alex was sleeping soundly. They talked for a few minutes regarding Alex's morning routine since it looked very unlikely that Kelly would be home by the time she waked. Poor baby. It would be incredibly hard on her if Nick didn't make it.

"Paging Dr. Riuski to ICU. Code blue. Code blue."

Kelly's heart slammed against the walls of her chest. It had to be Nick. He was having a medical emergency.

She flew to Nick's bedside. Mitchell was standing there, his mouth agape, his eyes wide. One nurse was injecting a vial of something into the IV. Another was pumping on Nick's chest.

"Oh, my God! No. No."

The screams came from Mitchell. Kelly grabbed him and held on to his arm as they watched the lines across the heart monitor flutter and then go flat.

Dr. Riuski rushed in and pushed through the frantic nurses to take over the task of trying to revive Nick. The taunting line running across the monitor stayed flat. In the prime of his life, on a night when he should have been basking in success, Nick Warner's heart had stopped beating.

Kelly's husband was dead.

Saturday, 4:15 a.m.
University of Colorado Hospital

KELLY HAD A LOT MORE inner resources than Jack had suspected. She didn't break down again, though Jack wondered if she were running on sheer nerves as she dealt with the immediate and pragmatic details of death. She was in the room where they'd met with Dr. Riuski earlier, finishing off the last of the paperwork before Nick's body could be released to the medical examiner for a full autopsy.

Mitchell was still here, too, waiting to talk to Kelly again. He'd been hanging out in the waiting room with his cell phone to his ear and apparently making sure that every entertainment editor in the country got their news flash concerning Nick's demise straight from the manager's mouth.

Jack was standing at the counter behind Kelly wrapping up a call to PPS. He'd talked to one of the night tech agents and asked him to add the news of Nick's death to Evangeline's daily report. By the time he broke the connection, the hospital halls were rocking.

"I have a right to get the news."

"You can't go in there, sir. This is a hospital."

"Like hell, I can't."

Jack ducked into the hall just as an insistent paparazzo with a camera knocked over a crash cart and
sent its contents clattering to the floor and rolling
down the hall. A nurse who could have lasted a few
bells in the ring with a heavyweight was standing in
front of the guy, trying to take his camera from him
while she blocked his entrance to the ICU where
Nick's body was still lying.

Jack rushed to the nurse's aid, grabbing the man's
arms and pinning him to the wall as she wrestled the
camera from him.

"Get your hands off me, jerk."

"As soon as you calm down."

"Where's Nick Warner? I know he's here."

"He's departed the building, and I suggest you do
the same, nicely, the way the nurse asked you to."

"I'm not the one causing trouble. I've got a right
to cover news events."

Jack flared his denim jacket and exposed his
weapon. "Your rights just got canceled. Now turn
around, walk back to the elevator and leave the hospital quietly."

"I have my credentials. I'm legitimate. You can't
shoot me for doing my job."

"He can't, but I can."

Jack looked up to see Gilly Carter walking toward
them from the stairwell. Carter stuck his ID in the
photographer's face. "Detective Carter with the
Denver Police."

Jack released the man. "Hail, hail, the gang's all here."

"Don't tell me you were hired to protect the victim," Carter mocked.

"No, the victims are never my clients. You should know that by now."

"Then why are you here?"

Jack waited until the disgruntled paparazzo had walked away, apparently heading for the elevator. "Mrs. Warner and her daughter are under PPS protection."

"Really. That must have happened after last night's murder."

"Nick called our office this morning."

"Is he talking tonight?"

"Not tonight or any other time. He died a few minutes ago."

Carter looked grim. "A high-profile murder during the highest-profile event of the year, and it would have to fall to me. Where's Mrs. Warner now?"

"She's signing some forms for the hospital, but she's pretty shook up."

"I'm sure. I'll go easy on her."

"You could wait until she's had a few hours sleep."

"And been briefed by you?"

"I'm not her attorney."

"Right, and you're not a cop, either. Try to remember both of those things. And since Mrs. Warner and I are both here, I think we should talk now."

"I was sure you would."

KELLY WAS BONE TIRED. She'd love to sink into a hot bath and close her burning eyes, but there was no avoiding Detective Carter. He'd suggested the hospital coffee shop for his informal questioning session.

As it turned out, that wasn't such a bad idea. The wait staff wasn't on duty at this hour of the morning and the refreshment came from impersonal chrome machines, which wouldn't be eavesdropping. This time Kelly had a cup of brew along with the detective and Jack—and Mitchell, who'd voluntarily joined them.

Kelly sat next to Mitchell. Jack sat across from her on the same side of the table as the detective, which made her feel a tad abandoned, as if Jack had morphed from confidant to authority figure.

The detective wasted no time in getting started with the questions. "Do you have any idea who shot your husband?"

"No," she answered, "except that I assume it was the same man who broke into our rented house last night."

"Your husband talked of a stalker. Do you have any notes the stalker had sent or any recordings of messages he may have left on you telephone?"

"Not that I know of. Nick gets stalked a lot. He loves…" She swallowed hard. "He *loved* to interact with fans, but he always said there were crazies out there who couldn't recognize limits. He took precautions, such as hiring security for the rented house, but he never seemed to think there was a real threat."

"What about you, Mr. Caruthers? Do you have the

names of any of the crazed fans who pushed the limits of the law to get to know Nick better?"

"No." Mitchell answered quickly, then buried his head in his hands for a few seconds before going on. "You'll have to excuse me. I'm still shaken, but I'll definitely look into any correspondence that may have gone through my office and see if anything suspicious pops up."

"I'd appreciate that. What about people he actually knew? Did he have enemies, anyone who you think might like to see him dead?"

"No." Kelly and Mitchell both answered at the same time, blurting out the answer with confidence.

"Everybody liked Nick," Mitchell insisted. "He was the life of the party, generous to a fault. He'd give you the shirt off his back—literally, even if the shirt happened to be a Borrelli." Mitchell smiled, then blinked repeatedly and wiped the cuff of his own shirt across his eyes. "I can't imagine that anyone would have reason to kill Nick."

"And yet someone did," Carter said. "What about love triangles? I know this isn't the best time to bring this up, but was it possible that Nick was involved with another woman?"

"Most definitely not," Mitchell asserted, shooting Kelly a warning look that she had no trouble deciphering. It was clear he wanted Nick's secret sex life to die with him.

So basically, Carter had asked the wrong question. Nick was not involved with another woman. Carter continued to fire questions at them for fifteen to twenty minutes. Kelly tried to cooperate with him, but fatigue set in to the point she could barely make sense of what he was asking.

Finally, the detective announced he'd covered enough for now, but that they should call him if they thought of anything that might help him make an arrest in the case.

"Does this mean you have no suspects in tonight's shooting?" Mitchell asked.

"Not at this time, but we still have lots of people to question and evidence to investigate. We'll get the perpetrator. It would just make it a lot easier if we had a motive."

Mitchell rested his arm across the back of Kelly's chair. "What about Kelly? Do you think she's still in danger?"

"Not likely," Carter admitted. "The guy could have hurt her when he broke into the house. He didn't, and he left fairly quickly when he realized her husband wasn't there. Looks to me as if the man was out to get Nick and he did. I'd say he's lying low right now or else he's on the run."

"That means it's no longer necessary for someone from PPS to be at her side every second." Mitchell turned to Jack. "You can consider your services terminated."

"That should be Mrs. Warner's decision," Carter said, then went into his spiel about the need for them to be available for questioning though it was permissible for them to return to Los Angeles. Jack stood when Carter made his departure, but didn't walk away.

Mitchell dropped his arm from the back of Kelly's chair and took her hand. His felt warm, which meant hers were cold, the same stinging cold that seemed to have penetrated the rest of her.

"I'll take care of having Nick's body shipped back to L.A. for burial," Mitchell said.

"You don't have to," she said. "I can do it."

"I know I don't have to. I'd like to help. Nick's death will be extremely difficult for Alex to handle, and you'll need to focus your time and attention on her. Do you want me to be there when she wakes up to help you through delivering the heartbreaking news?"

"No. I appreciate the offer, but I can handle it."

"At least let me drive you back to the hotel."

"I'll drive her," Jack countered.

"No use bothering you with that. I'm staying at the same hotel," Mitchell said.

Kelly felt as if the two men were fighting over her, though neither really wanted her. "I'll ride with Jack, but I'll call you tomorrow."

"Fine." Mitchell scooted his chair away from the table quickly, as if he no longer chose to be that near her. "You have my number."

"Programmed into my cell."

Jack stayed silent as Mitchell stood and strode away, leaving only her and Jack in the deserted coffee shop. "I guess we should go," she said.

"Whenever you're ready."

She was ready now, but she had the eerie feeling as she stepped away from the table that the nightmare that had started last night with the shooting of the guard had not ended with Nick's death.

She prayed her instincts were wrong.

Saturday, 5:38 a.m.
Denver Hotel

DAWN WAS FAST FADING into the golden hues of daylight as Jack pulled PSS's black escort car into the valet parking lane in front of the hotel. He glanced over at Kelly. Her eyes were swollen and rimmed in dark circles and mascara dripped down her cheeks like black tears. She'd kicked out of her shoes, and sat slumped against the seat, one foot propped on the dash. Even the paparazzi would have had difficulty recognizing her like this.

"I'm a mess," she said, when she caught him staring.

"You're not so bad." The sad truth was her vulnerability was even more powerful an aphrodisiac then her incredible beauty had been at the premiere.

The valet opened Kelly's door. She waved him away and made no move to get out. "I know that Mitchell and Carter agreed it was unnecessary, but I'd feel better if you stayed on duty awhile longer— for Alex's sake."

He reached across the seat and took her hand, then was immediately sorry that he had. The touch unleashed a rush of memories and produced that increasingly familiar burning sensation deep in his gut.

"I'm all yours as long as you need me."

"That will be until I can get a flight back to Los Angeles. With Mitchell taking care of the transfer of the body, there's no reason for me to stay in Denver any longer than necessary, and I'd like to take Alex home before I tell her about her father's death."

"Makes sense. I'll drive you to the airport."

"Deal."

He'd drive her to the airport, and that would be it. She'd go back to her palatial mansion in Beverly Hills. He'd stay in Denver. She'd been out of his league fourteen years ago. She still was. Besides, she already had her passions.

All he had to do was manage to keep his lips from touching hers for a few more hours. That could well be the most difficult part of this assignment.

Chapter Five

Kelly had dropped into bed the minute she'd hit her hotel room, but as exhausted as she was, sleep had eluded her. Lying in the dark, the events of the past few hours had seemed more nightmare than reality, and she half expected to hear Nick open the door and walk into the suite at any minute.

Less than two hours after she'd fallen into a restless sleep the phone rang. Nick's only living relative, a sister in Kansas whom he hadn't seen in years had been the first to call. She wanted to know if she was in his will. Kelly's parents' call had followed and they had been significantly more upset by the murder. They'd pleaded with Kelly to fly to their house instead of going home.

The offer was tempting, but Kelly couldn't revert into childhood to avoid responsibility. When Alex woke up, she'd stopped answering the phone and set the TV controls so that all Alex could watch were the videos they'd brought with them. Still, it was a struggle to keep Alex from hearing the news before Kelly was ready to explain it all to her.

Mitchell had recommended chartering a private jet and then taken care of the details for her. They were on their way to the airport now, Alex in the backseat, Jack at the wheel.

"Look, Mommy. It's snowing."

Kelly stared at the first flakes falling from the dull gray sky and watched them melt on the windshield. "You're right."

"Can I play in it? Can I, Mommy?"

"Not today."

"Why?"

"We have an airplane waiting for us. We have to go home."

"Why isn't Daddy going home with us?"

"He's busy." She hated lying to Alex, but she wouldn't have to do it much longer. She turned to face Jack. "How much farther to the airport?"

"About twenty miles."

"I haven't seen any signs."

"It's a small one, just used by a few cargo planes and private jets. It's always busy, though."

"It must cater to a lot of skiers since it's so close to the mountains."

"Quite a few, but some of the smaller planes land closer to the slopes."

"Do you still ski?" she asked, remembering that he was an avid skier his one winter on Lake Tahoe.

"I ski when I can. The job and the ranch keep me busy."

"You have a ranch?" For some reason that surprised her, but then she didn't actually know anything about his life for the last fourteen years, or for that matter, the eighteen years before that.

"The Single S. It's not too far from here—as the crow flies."

"And I guess you still ride a Harley."

He shook his head. "Gave up the Harley when I went into the army and never got back to it. I have a couple of four-wheelers and about a dozen horses I ride on the ranch, and a black Wrangler for the highway—when I'm not driving a PPS vehicle."

"Can I ride your horses?" Alex piped up from the backseat.

"Sure," Jack said. "Next time you're in Denver."

"Goody. Can we come back to Denver tomorrow, Mommy?"

"Not tomorrow, sweetie."

Alex grunted her disapproval and twisted her mouth into her well-practiced pout. Kelly's emotions sank even lower as she was struck by how different Alex's tomorrow would be. At four, she wouldn't fully understand death, but she'd know enough to hurt. Her daughter's grief would break Kelly's heart.

Jack turned off the Interstate onto a two-lane paved road. They rode in silence for the next few miles and Kelly stared at the unfamiliar scenery while her mind seemed to jump from one thought to another. Finding a burial spot. Details about the funeral. All the legal aspects. There was a will, but she couldn't remember the provisions except that Nick had included adequate provisions for her to take care of Alex if he died before she was grown.

The scenery changed. A rolling pasture stretched off to the right, dotted with cattle and a few wild pear and hackberry trees with snow just starting to stick to their bare branches. A sign on a gate they passed said Twisting River Ranch.

"What made you decide to get into ranching?"

Jack didn't answer, and when she looked over at him, she realized he was intensely focused on a low black car that was coming toward them at breakneck speed. Then, all of a sudden, the car slowed down.

"Get out of your seat belt and hit the floor, Alex," Jack ordered. "You, too, Kelly. Do it now!"

Kelly unloosed her seat belt while her mind struggled to comprehend what was going on. And then she saw what looked to be an assault rifle slide past the driver-side window of the approaching vehicle. Panic hit so hard and so fast, she could barely breathe.

"Hurry, Alex. It's a game. First one to the floor wins." She dived over the seat, her feet flying in the air, one of them making contact with Jack's head. She pulled Alex to the floor with her.

Jack swerved the car, leaving the highway and taking off across the bumpy terrain. Kelly's pulse was racing, keeping tune with the cacophony of gunfire and the sound of bullets hammering into the car.

"Are you two okay?" Jack's voice echoed around her.

"Yes. Are you?"

"Yeah. Hang on."

They hit a deep rut, and she flew into the air and back onto Alex. Alex started crying. "Get off of me, Mommy. I don't like this game."

"It's like riding a wild bronc," Jack said. "Be over before you know it."

Kelly tried to keep her weight off her daughter but she wasn't too successful with the car jerking and bouncing along the rough stretch of pasture. She held on and prayed until the car finally came to a screeching halt, not realizing until then that the gunfire had ceased.

"All's clear," Jack said. "Now tell me that wasn't exciting."

Kelly lifted her battered body off of Alex. The sight of the shattered window next to Jack sent a new and chilling wave of fear to her heart.

Jack opened the door and started to climb out."

"Where are you going?"

"To survey the damage."

"No. Let's just get out of here. Now. Please, Jack, hurry before they come back."

"They won't come back, at least not now. It's not how the game is played."

"I don't like this game," Alex complained again.

"Me, either," Kelly agreed as she helped Alex off the floorboard. "Me, either."

Kelly didn't fully trust Jack's assessment that the shooters were gone, and she had no desire to see the evidence of how close they'd come to getting shot. But when seconds ticked by and there was no sign of the black car, the shuddering eased—at least on the outside.

She turned the handle and opened the back door. "Stay inside the car, Alex," Kelly said, desperately trying for a steady voice and not quite making it.

"I want to play with the snow."

"Not yet."

Kelly tweaked her daughter's nose as playfully as she could manage and climbed out of the car, shutting the door behind her so that Alex wouldn't hear her conversation with Jack. She walked around to the back where he was examining a nearly flat tire.

"We could have been killed back there."

"You think?"

His flippant response didn't match his tone or the concern etched into every line of his face. "Who was shooting at us?"

"You tell me, Kelly."

"Do you think I know?"

"What the hell was your husband involved with?"

"Nothing. Nick wasn't involved with anything criminal. Why do you think that?"

"Because stalkers don't hire a professional hit

man to take out the wife and kid of the object of their obsession."

"A hit man?"

"That wasn't road rage back there, not with an AK-47."

"What are you insinuating?"

"That either someone just tried to take you out or that was a hell of a goodbye party he threw you."

"Why do you assume that was about me? Carter told you that there's no reason to think I'm in danger."

"Is that a fact?"

"Did you ever think that might have been about you, Jack Sanders? Maybe it was someone with a grudge against you—or else the gunman made a mistake and fired on the wrong car?"

"It was no mistake, and it was about you."

As much as she hated to admit it, she knew Jack was probably right. A hit man. Her knees went weak, and when she leaned against the back fender for support, her fingers fell into a hole where the metal had been torn off by a bullet. A bullet that could have… "He could have killed Alex."

"He could have killed all of us."

"Especially you. We were on the floorboard, but you were driving. I don't see how the bullet that shattered the window kept from hitting you in the head."

"The windows on this car are bulletproof. A direct hit at close range might have still taken them out, but the shooter couldn't get a direct hit once we left the highway and started swerving through the pasture."

She looked around nervously. "If that was a hit man, then how can you be so sure he won't come back and finish the job?"

"Strikes like that are meant to be quick and come as a total surprise, so that the shooter can disappear before anyone sees him in the area. Nine times out of ten the victim doesn't react fast enough to keep from being as riddled with bullets as this car.

Nine times out of ten.

That's how close they'd come to being a crime statistic. The difference had been Jack's instant response to the danger. She studied him as he struggled to open the damaged trunk, his muscles straining against the fabric of his cotton shirt.

He'd changed tremendously over the years, though she wasn't sure she'd realized just how much until this second. He'd been incredibly virile then, but wild and reckless.

He was still incredibly virile, but now he was levelheaded and pure hero. "I don't know how to thank you."

He met her gaze. "Thank me by telling me what's going on."

"I would if I knew. Believe me, I would."

He stepped toward her and his hand closed around her right wrist. "Then let me keep protecting you while we find out."

"I have to go back to L.A. I have to bury Nick."

"Nick's dead. You can't save him. It's you and Alex you have to think about now."

Right now staying in Denver was the last thing she wanted to do. All the problems were here. If she could just get back to their estate in Beverly Hills, life would return to normal.

But the rational part of her knew that was only wishful thinking and faulty reasoning. If someone had hired a hit man to kill her, the danger wouldn't stop just because she caught a plane to Los Angeles.

It all came down to this: did she dare put hers and Alex's life in Jack's hands?

"I don't want to go back to that hotel," she said. "I don't want to be around all of those people in town for the film festival."

"You don't have to. You and Alex can stay at the Single S." Jack put his hands on her shoulders. "Look at me, Kelly. I only want to protect you, and I can do that better here in Denver where I already know all the parameters."

She tilted her head and met his gaze. "If we stay on your ranch, it will just be for protection."

"I didn't offer anything else."

But there was something else between them, maybe only sparks from the fires of passion they'd shared that one night so long ago. But if she went with him, the sparks might ignite. And then where would she be?

Alive, which she wouldn't have been if Jack hadn't been driving them to the airport today.

"Okay, Jack. To the Single S it is."

He dropped his hands from her shoulders. "Right after I change this flat."

She was calmer as she stepped back into the car, though plenty of adrenaline still raced through her veins. She had no idea what she was up against, but by some quirk of fate, she'd ended up in the hands of Jack Sanders. Right now she couldn't imagine that there was any better place to be.

Saturday, 2:42 p.m.
The Single S

JACK PULLED UP at the door to his house with Kelly and Alex and was forced to admit to himself that it was a tad less impressive than he liked to believe. He'd bought it with the acreage and outbuildings a year after he'd taken the job with PPS.

He'd settled in the way a man does. He marked his territory by fixing fences and gates and upgrading the stables, hay barns and ranching equipment. The house he'd pretty much left as it was except for filling the shelves with his books and the refrigerator with his beer.

They were accosted by his two overly friendly Labrador retrievers and his new collie puppy as they stepped out of the car. The dogs made quick friends of the new female guests and had collected lots of cooing and petting before he could get the door unlocked.

"It's not much," Jack said. Actually it seemed a lot less now that he was here with Kelly. The rugs were old, the original plank floors were marred and the wood and leather furniture was worn. There were no curtains at the windows, and no pictures on the wall, except a print of an Indian warrior the previous owner had left.

Jack had seen photos once of the Beverly Hills estate Kelly and Nick owned. There had been a full spread in one of their receptionist's fanzines. Six bedrooms, two pools, probably servants at her beck and call and fresh flowers in every room. What in the world had he been thinking to bring her here?

Thinking of her protection, he reminded himself, and it really didn't matter what she thought of his living arrangements. Still, he stopped to straighten the newspapers he'd left scattered over the sofa and grabbed a pair of dirty socks he'd left in the middle of the floor. "Sorry for the mess."

"You weren't exactly expecting your clients to come home with you."

"No, this is a first." It had never even occurred to him with any of the others.

"What's your puppy's name?" Alex asked.

"Stormy. And the big dogs are Pete and Repeat."

"Repeat. That's funny." Alex spotted his prizewinning rainbow trout that was mounted and hanging over the stone fireplace. "You got a fish."

"I sure do. Do you like to go fishing?"

She made a face. "I'm too little to go fishing."

"No one's too little to fish."

"Can I touch it?"

"Sure." Jack swooped Alex up in his arms and held her so that she was eye to eye with the trout.

She touched it warily, then jerked her hand back. "Will it bite?"

"No. Feel it all you want. You can't hurt it, and it can't hurt you."

Kelly ran her hand along the edge of the rough-hewn mantel. "How long have you lived here?"

"A couple of years. Guess I should have fixed the house up more by now."

"No, it's fine."

"It works for me."

She scanned the room while she unzipped Alex's parka. "I can see how it would. It looks like you in a way."

"Unkempt?"

"You are anything but unkempt, Jack Sanders. I meant solid, tough but unpredictable—and interesting."

"Tough and unpredictable. I doubt I could score with that resume on PickUpHotChicks.com."

"You're kidding. There's no such Web site, is there?"

"I doubt it." He shrugged out of his jacket and held out his hand for Alex's. "I'll hang these on the hook by the back door."

"Wait, and you can take mine, too." He held the collar of her fur-trimmed leather trench coat while she slipped out of it, fully aware that it probably cost more than his whole wardrobe.

A nail on the wall by the back door didn't seem appropriate for expensive leather and fur, so he took the coats to his bedroom and tossed all three of them on top of his faded quilt. When he returned to the den, Alex was playing with pieces of fatwood from the basket on the hearth and Kelly was standing at the window behind the rectangular oak table he used as a desk.

"I love the view."

"That's Fulman's River. Great fishing."

She nodded. "I tried fly-fishing once. I wasn't good at it, but I could probably learn."

He pictured her in his river, her hair blowing in a spring breeze, the silvery spray wetting her jeans. His throat clogged. "It's not for everyone."

Kelly stepped back from the window. "Is there somewhere we can talk?"

"The kitchen. I'll make a pot of coffee."

"Where's Stormy?" Alex asked as they walked away from her.

"He's outside with the other dogs," Kelly answered. "Stay in here and play with the wood while Jack and I talk business, and when we're through I'll take you outside to see him."

"And the other dogs, too?"

"Right. We'll see all the dogs."

Jack was filling the pot with fresh water when Kelly grabbed her cell phone from her pocket. He hadn't heard it ring, but then she'd had it on vibrate all day and had been screening her calls and ignoring most of them.

"It's Detective Carter," she said. "Do you want to explain what happened? You seem to have a better understanding of the hit man angle than I do."

"You talk first, and then I'll add my spin on the attack."

She nodded and took the call.

"WE'VE MADE AN ARREST."

Kelly must have misunderstood the detective. "Are you saying you've arrested the man who murdered Nick?"

"Who *allegedly* murdered Nick. But he's a strong suspect. He's been in and out of mental hospitals for the last five years and he has a history of stalking famous politicians and entertainers."

"Did he know Nick?"

"Not before last night. He spotted him at a local hotspot when he was out cruising clubs in hopes of running into celebrities."

"And he shot him just because he could?"

"He says he tried to talk to Nick and Nick brushed him off. He got angry and when Nick left that club to meet friends at another club just down the way, the suspect followed him. At that point, he claims Nick pulled a gun and that the fatal shots were fired in a scuffle to disarm Nick."

"You're saying the shooting was self-defense?"

"There was no weapon on Nick. That's why the suspect's in jail."

"But he told you that's what happened?"

"We pieced some of it together, but he's confessed to everything."

So if Carter had the man in jail who'd killed

Nick, then who had just shot at them? "When did you arrest this man?"

"A couple of hours ago. He called the station and told the clerk on phone duty that he'd killed a man. That's all he'd say. She put in a call to the patrol team in the area and when they arrived at the address he'd given her, he was waiting for them with his hands out to be handcuffed."

"What's the name of the suspect?"

"We haven't released his name to the media yet, but we will soon so I may as well tell you. It's David Bates."

Bates, like the famous psycho. But she doubted psychos hired hit men.

"Guess that's it," the detective said. "I'll get in touch with you if we need anything else. Are you and your daughter flying back to L.A. today?"

"We were—until someone tried to kill us."

"What?"

"We were fired on from a passing car by a man with an AK-47."

"You're kidding, right?"

"Do you think I would kid about that after what happened to Nick?"

Carter muttered a curse. "Excuse the French. This town's gone crazy. Can you identify the shooter?"

"No."

"Did you get his license plate number?"

"No, it happened too fast."

"Are you still with Jack Sanders?"

"He was driving the car. He's standing right here if you'd like to talk to him."

"Put him on."

She handed Jack the phone, more confused than ever. She couldn't believe Nick had become involved in anything that would get him killed let alone put a hit man on her trail. But if he'd been killed by David Bates, then who had fired on them? And how long would it be before the assault-rifle hoodlum made another attempt to take her out?

She had to get out of here, maybe take Alex and leave the country, go anyplace where she could keep her safe. She tried to listen to Jack's end of the conversation, but frightening scenarios were clouding her mind.

She checked on Alex. The little darling had put all the fatwood back in the basket and was pushing her little foot into one of the boots Jack had left drying near the hearth. Kelly poured herself a cup of the fresh-brewed coffee and walked to the kitchen window, staying close so she could hear Jack's end of the conversation. His voice rose.

"You can do what you want, but I'm not letting either Kelly or Alex out of my sight until I know who's really behind this, and it's not that fruitcake you have in jail now."

In spite of everything, she felt a twinge of relief. Who'd have ever expected that the renegade rebel who'd taken her on the most thrilling midnight ride

of her life would be the man she'd count on when her
world became steeped in danger?

She took another sip of the coffee and felt the
tenseness that knotted her muscles start to ease. The
relief lasted only a second, until Kelly heard the front
door open and slam shut. She raced to the den,
sloshing coffee all over her slacks and the kitchen
floor.

She scanned the room quickly. Alex was nowhere in sight.

Chapter Six

Kelly rushed to the front door, yanked it open, and then fell against the facing as the panic melted into crippling relief and an outburst of fear-induced anger.

She raced to Alex, who was trying her best to hug the wiggling collie, and stooped so that they were at eye level. "You know not to go outside without permission, Alex."

Alex turned away, and Kelly grabbed her arm and pulled her back to face her. "You are never, *ever* to leave any house without asking. You have to do as I say. Do you understand me?"

Alex started to sob, and Kelly let go of her as the three dogs stared at her with accusing eyes. Even they knew she'd lost it. The events of the last twenty-four hours had turned her into a hysterical, paranoid shrew. "I'm sorry, Alex. I didn't mean to sound so angry."

"I just wanted to see the horseys. See?" Alex pointed a shaky finger at two beautiful animals in a fenced area a few yards from where they were standing.

Jack extended a hand to help Kelly from her stooped position. She hadn't realized he was there, but of course he would be. He took his job as body-guard very seriously, but even he couldn't protect them against everything. She'd panicked over noth-ing, but it would have taken only that split second for someone to have walked into the house and abducted her daughter.

"I'll get our coats and hats, and then we'll go see the horses together," she offered.

Alex sniffled and rubbed her wet eyes with the backs of her little curled fists. Kelly pulled a clean tissue from her pocket and held it to Alex's nose. "Blow," she instructed, with a voice still strained from the latest fright.

Alex blew and went back to playing with Stormy, her tears forgotten.

"I'll get your coats," Jack said.

When he returned with them, she helped Alex into hers and then started to follow Alex as she skipped away with the collie at her heels. Jack took her arm and held her back.

"I know," she said, stuffing her arms though the sleeves of her coat. "I overreacted, but something could have happened to Alex. Anyone could have come through the gate to your ranch. It's not even locked."

"The gates are locked."

"I didn't see you lock or unlock them when we came in. They just swung open when you stopped near them." She jerked from his grasp. "I'm not questioning your ability as a bodyguard, but you're not some fictional hero with superhuman powers."

"I'm not a hero, fictional or otherwise, but I do have superhuman powers. Only difference is that mine come from technology instead of incredible abilities on my part."

"What kind of technology?"

"Motion detectors, silent alarms that go straight to my cell phone, hidden cameras at key positions around the property and house. I knew the second the door opened that Alex had opened it."

Jack pulled a handheld device the size of a small cell phone from his pocket. He pushed a key and the recorded image of Alex slipping out the door and being accosted by Stormy's welcoming tongue and wagging tail flashed across the digital monitor.

"Why would you have that kind of equipment on your ranch? Is it that dangerous to live here?"

"The equipment belongs to PPS. We're experimenting with it for use in a safe house we're developing."

"Having your own safe house seems a bit extreme for a bodyguard service."

"We're not just a bodyguard service. We specialize in protection and investigation. Anyone can hire us, but many of our clients are top executives, foreign dignitaries and former politicians who've become targets from enemies as well organized as the Mafia or terrorist groups. Occasionally we interact with Homeland Security. The world is a very volatile place right now."

Jack hooked his thumbs in his pockets and kicked at a lump of mud with the toe of his boot. "You're safer on this ranch than anyplace else in Colorado. I just need to alert my boss at PPS as to what's going on and get Lenny working on discovering what Nick was into."

Names, places, technology—they were all coming at her too fast. "Who's Lenny?"

"PPS's favorite resident geek. His real name's William Lennard, and if it's in cyberspace, he can find it."

"Nick wasn't involved in anything criminal, Jack. I'm sure of it. He had his faults, but a man as worried as he was about the public finding out he was a homosexual certainly wouldn't have dabbled in anything illegal. He wouldn't have risked his career for that."

"Drugs are illegal, and Nick had amphetamines in his system the night he was killed," Jack reminded her, as they started walking toward where Alex was standing and staring through the fence at a golden palomino with a white tail and flowing mane.

"Then someone slipped them into his drinks. That was his weakness. Drinking and partying with his friends."

Jack nodded, but she could tell he wasn't convinced.

"Can I ride the horsey, Mommy? Please. Please."

Jack lifted Alex and set her atop his shoulders. "What do you think, Mom? Shall we take a short ride before the snow starts up again? Somebody I know could use a relaxing break."

Murder and assault rifles. Danger and sophisticated surveillance technology. All the makings of one of Nick's movies, only the starring role was played by the very virile and sexy Jack Sanders in jeans and a denim jacket, snowflakes shimmering in his dark hair, her daughter laughing atop his shoulders.

"Sure. Cowboy up!" she said, using an expression from one of Nick's movies while she high-fived her daughter. She wasn't quite sure what it meant, but she thought it had something to do with smiling when you felt like hiding under a huge rock.

Alex clapped her hands and dug her knees into Jack's ribs to keep her balance on his shoulders.

"Alex and I can ride on the palomino," Jack said, "since she's already taken to Ishwar."

"That's an unusual name for a horse." Though unusual names fit in this strange, surreal world of high tech and horses.

"It's an Indian word. I'm not sure what it means, but I like the sound of it."

"We'll need to change clothes," Kelly said, looking down at her Manolo Blahnik strapped boots with their four-inch heels.

Jack set Alex back on the ground. "I'll make that

phone call to PPS and get the horses saddled while you get into riding gear. Dress warm. That wind can cut right through you if we get up to a good gallop."

Alex ran toward the house with three dogs running circles around her short legs. Kelly walked behind her slowly, her heart warming at the sight of her daughter's innocent excitement. Too bad her life couldn't stay that way forever.

But nothing ever did. Her own life was proof of that. A promising career that had nose-dived before it began. Her seemingly perfect marriage that had ended in disillusionment and tragedy.

Her night of skyrockets in flight so long ago with Jack Sanders—and she definitely wasn't going there now. Sex and assault rifles were not a good mix.

KELLY'S SORREL CANTERED next to the palomino in a scene that could have come straight from a Norman Rockwell painting. Jack seemed bigger than life in the saddle, taller than he looked on foot, masculine and commanding.

Alex, on the other hand, looked more petite than ever, with her tiny hands lying over Jack's larger ones. He was good with kids. She wondered if he missed not having any of his own.

Or maybe he had children. He didn't wear a wedding band, and the ranch showed no signs of a woman's touch, but that didn't mean he hadn't ever been married.

The thought bothered her, and she pushed it from

her mind. Unfortunately the thoughts that took its place were even more disturbing.

She hadn't been on a horse, but on the back of Jack's Harley the night they'd taken the wild ride up Canyon Road. She'd pressed against his back as he'd taken the sharp curves, going dangerously fast on an all-but-deserted mountain road.

But the hammering of her heart had nothing to do with fear. Her hormones had been literally exploding inside her, and she'd thought she'd die from the thrill of it all.

A thrill she didn't need now. She pushed her sorrel into a gallop, and threw her sexual frustrations into the ride and the biting wind in her face. She didn't know where she was going and didn't really care. She just held on and let the sorrel run.

When the horse finally stopped, she was as out of breath as if she'd been doing the work. Breathless, but feeling much better than she had minutes ago. The exhilarating ride had dissolved some of the tension, leaving her warm yet tingly on the inside.

She had no idea how to get back to the ranch house, but she knew Jack and Alex would show up soon. With the high-tech equipment he had on the Single S, he could probably track and find a beetle.

She dismounted and tied her mount, then stretched and took off her gloves. Her stomach growled, reminding her she hadn't eaten since last night's dinner. Luckily she'd thrown together some food while Alex had dallied at putting on her warm socks and boots.

Just as Kelly started unpacking the fare, she heard a neigh followed by Alex's high-pitched laughter.

"What took you guys so long?" she teased as Jack dismounted and helped Alex from the palomino.

"We would have hurried if we'd known there was food waiting."

"Just sandwiches," she said. "Are you hungry?"

"I'm a man. I'm always hungry."

"What kind of sandwich?" Alex asked, always a little anxious about what she might be asked to eat.

"Peanut butter and jelly, what else?"

"Goody."

Jack's eyebrows arched. "Did you find that in my cupboard?"

"No, your choices were limited to potato chips and microwave popcorn. I always carry the essentials when I travel with Alex. Even the most luxurious and costly hotels don't always have the staples required by a four-year-old."

"Nice thing about being a cowboy," Jack said. "The restaurants at even the cheapest hotels usually have beer."

"So you're a beer man?"

"Pretty much. Maybe a bourbon now and then, but none of that fancy stuff with umbrellas bobbing around in the glass." He looped Ishwar's reins around the limb of a hackberry tree near where Kelly had tied the sorrel.

"There's a creek just beyond those trees and some softer earth," Jack said. "It's a great picnic spot."

"Lead on."

Kelly surveyed the area, then spread the large napkins from her bag as makeshift place mats. Alex's sandwich was cut into four triangles the way she liked it. The other two sandwiches were halved. Jack pulled three bottled waters from his knapsack and placed one on each napkin.

"Cool," she said. "Always nice to have something to rinse the peanut butter from the roof of my mouth."

Jack dropped to the cold ground and propped his back against the trunk of a tree. "There's a market close to PPS headquarters that delivers. You can make a list on the way into town, and the groceries will be ready and waiting when we head back to the ranch."

Apprehension hit again. "I didn't realize we'd be leaving the ranch."

"Just a quick trip to PPS."

"I'm still recovering from our last trip."

"There won't be a repeat."

"How can you be so sure?"

"The perp will need time to regroup, and there's a secret back entrance from the ranch along back roads. No one will see us leave and no one will know our schedule. It would be all but impossible to intercept us."

"You do think of everything, don't you?"

"Right, so trust me."

She was trying, but the thought of getting back in his car set her nerves on edge. "Time to eat, Alex," she called, suddenly ready to get this picnic over with.

"I'm coming, Mommy." But Alex made no move
to join them. Instead she picked up a rock and looked
under it, no doubt at some squirming bugs. Adventure had always been more appealing to Alex than
food, and she got little opportunity for adventure
such as this.

"Don't wander out of my sight, and don't get too
near the stream. It's much too cold to get wet."

"Maybe the stream wasn't such a good idea," Jack
said.

"I'm not sure my going to PPS headquarters is,
either. In fact, I don't see the point of it."

"It was Evangeline's suggestion, but I agree
with her."

"And who is Evangeline?"

"The head honcho of PPS. She and her husband
are the ones who started the business."

"So why isn't he at least co-head honcho?"

"Robert Prescott was in a small private plane that
went down in Spain two years ago when he was on a
business trip. They never found his body or that of the
friend he was with, but they were both assumed dead."

"I'm surprised she kept the business. I mean you
usually think of men when you think of bodyguards."

"She not only kept it, she's turned it into one of
the premiere security groups in the country. Like I
said, she's into the high-tech aspect of protection
and investigation, and I'd have to differ with you on
the male aspect of the business. We have some terrific female agents."

"Like Sara Montgomery?"

"Right on, and Evangeline herself."

"Did Evangeline remarry?"

"No. I don't think she's had a date since Robert died. She seldom talks about him, but it's obvious she still really misses him. Sometimes I think she's holding on to some kind of far-fetched hope that he's still alive. Anyway, you'll like Evangeline. Everyone does."

"So why does she think I need to come into your headquarters?"

"To help Lenny get started on his research."

"What will he be looking for?"

"Whatever turns up. I'm partial to fieldwork myself, but it's amazing what Lenny can turn up without ever leaving his desk. There's a lot of private information floating around in cyberspace, some hidden behind passwords or firewalls, but some only minimally protected."

"I still don't see how I can help. I don't know any of Nick's passwords."

"But you'll be the most likely person to know if something like bank accounts or purchases or investments look suspicious."

"Not necessarily. I know almost nothing about Nick's financial status. I hate to admit it, but I never thought much about money, except from a spending standpoint. I had unlimited charge accounts at every store on Rodeo Drive. Not that I spent all my time shopping. I stayed busy."

"With your own passions?"

"Right, and with caring for Alex. You'll have to go to our accountants in Los Angeles for account numbers or names of banks. That would be Powell and Powell."

"Do you and Nick have joint bank accounts?"

"Definitely not. None of our finances are joint. I signed a prenuptial agreement. They're common in the entertainment world."

"Do you know the name of Nick's attorney?

"Greg Carrolton. But you should also talk to Mitchell. He's a control freak, and Nick was his primary client. He probably knows the serial number on all three of Nick's sports cars by heart."

"We'll talk to Mitchell, but he didn't seem inclined to cooperate with me last night. Don't worry, though, you'll be more help than you think in establishing the initial search criteria. Lenny will ask the right questions, you'll just have to answer."

"Okay, I'll go with you today, but I'm not making any promises after that."

Kelly's phone rang, and the sudden noise startled her so that she jumped and knocked over her bottle of water, spilling it onto her napkin. Jack grabbed it before it soaked the remaining half of her sandwich, and Alex came running to get in on the excitement of a spill.

The caller ID indicated it was Mitchell. "Hello," she said, standing and walking away so that she could talk freely without upsetting Alex.

"Where are you?" Mitchell asked. "I just got a call from the pilot. He said you didn't show up."

"We ran into complications."

"Like what?"

"We were on our way to the airport when this black car came out of nowhere." He was silent while she explained the frightening ordeal and how Jack's swift actions had saved their lives.

"I don't understand this."

"Neither do I, Mitchell, but it happened. Jack thinks it was a hit man, likely hired by whomever killed Nick—or had him killed. He believes Nick was involved in something that put him on a target list."

"That's preposterous. No one *had* Nick killed. He just got drunk and wandered into the wrong area of town. Where are you now?"

Apparently he hadn't heard about David Bates's arrest. "I'm at Jack's ranch."

"Why on earth would you be there?"

"We need a place to talk and decide what I should do now."

"That's a pretty simple decision. You need to call Detective Carter and have him get you to the airport safely. I'll charter another flight."

"I'm not sure I'm ready to go back to Los Angeles."

"What else would you do? You have a husband to bury. And you need to make some kind of statement to the press and to Nick's grieving fans."

She exhaled slowly as the frustration and responsibilities weighed down on her. "I guess everyone knows about the murder by now."

"Of course they know. Haven't you been watching TV? Crowds are pouring into the streets around your estate and leaving flowers, candles, most any kind of remembrance you can imagine."

"I've been avoiding the news. I haven't talked to Alex about Nick."

"You have to tell her. If you don't, she'll hear it from someone else. It's only a matter of time."

"I know. It's just that things are so confusing right now. I'm in no shape to deal with her grief and I don't want to tell her when she's in a strange place and sleeping in a strange bed."

"Which is another reason why you need to go home. And you need to get away from Jack Sanders."

"What's that supposed to mean?"

"You're vulnerable, and I don't want him to take advantage of you."

"Our relationship is strictly about protection."

"I'm neither blind nor stupid, Kelly. I saw the way the two of you looked at each other when he arrived at the hotel yesterday and you were clinging to him last night while your husband was dying."

"I was in shock."

"You're not in shock now. So go back to Beverly Hills where you belong. I'll hire a protection service there. They'll have more training, anyway. It is California, after all."

It was no use to argue with Mitchell. He made good points. But could she tolerate flashbulbs popping in her face every time she looked out a window or opened a door when she was trying to stay alive— and more importantly, keep Alex alive?

"I'm sorry, Mitchell. I can't go home just yet."

"You're making a mistake."

"It won't be my first."

"Nick was a good man, Kelly. He wasn't much of a husband, I know, but he loved you in his own way and he worshipped Alex. Jack Sanders is wrong. Nick would never have become involved in anything that would have put either you or Alex in danger."

"I hope you're right, but someone killed Nick and those were real bullets flying around us this afternoon."

"If you keep hanging out with Jack, it will only give substance to the rumors that Nick was gay, and he never wanted that getting out."

Her patience ran out. "For crying out loud, Mitch ell. Let it go. Nick is dead. The rumors no longer matter—if they ever did."

"Don't dishonor your husband with some old fling, Kelly. That's all I'm asking."

"Goodbye, Mitchell." Snowflakes stuck to her face as she walked back to where Jack and Alex were standing by the horses.

"It's snowing again, Mommy."

Kelly only nodded.

"I can catch one. See." She put her face up and stuck out her tongue. "Jack teached me that."

Jack's gaze sought hers. "You okay?"

"Not really. That was Mitch."

"Did you ask him about helping with the investigation?"

"No, bad timing for that."

"What's wrong?"

"He's still insisting I fly back to Los Angeles today."

"And?"

"I told him I couldn't."

Jack reached across and wiped a snowflake from her eyelashes. "You made the right decision."

She hoped she had—for all their sakes. It would be truly pathetic if her reasoning had anything to do with a high school crush.

But there was no denying Jack was getting to her. And after four years of doing without any kind of intimacy, she wasn't sure how much willpower she had left.

Saturday, 5:34 p.m.
Parking garage at PPS

JACK STEERED into his reserved parking spot and pulled the gear into Park. He still couldn't think of how close he'd come to losing Kelly and Alex that afternoon without his chest caving in on him.

Let it go. Stay in the present. Focus on the immediate. It was the cardinal rule of protection.

The second rule, unfortunately, was to never get emotionally involved with the person you're hired to protect. Ethically, he should have Kelly assigned to a new agent. Realistically, there was no way he'd turn her protection over to anyone else.

Not after what Lenny had already learned. Jack

hated to hit Kelly with it, but he had no choice. She was already unbuckled and getting out of the car. The ugly truth was only minutes away.

Chapter Seven

The headquarters for Prescott Personal Securities took up the entire top floor of an impressive glass-and-steel skyscraper in downtown Denver. Kelly's first impression when she stepped out of the elevator and peered through the glass wall was that Evangeline, or her decorator, had excellent taste in office decor. Her second thought was that Evangeline had terrible taste in receptionists.

"Who's the goth queen?" she asked as they approached the door.

"Oh, that's Angel. Our own little Angel of Death."

Kelly stopped in her tracks. "What?"

"Sorry, bad timing. Her name's Angel. One of the guys pinned the nickname on her one day when she was looking particularly gruesome, and it stuck."

"So she actually works here?"

"She gives work a shot. I wouldn't say she's good at it. She's one of Evangeline's projects, but she grows on you. Place seems kind of dead when she's on vacation."

"A project?"

"I'll explain later." He stopped and peered into a rectangular box hung at eye level next to the door. A second later the double glass doors slid open.

"Is that an eye scan?"

"It is, but you and Alex have clearance by virtue of being with me."

"What if I weren't with you?"

"Then Angel would have to buzz you in—or not—depending on whether your business here was legitimate."

Alex headed straight for the huge floor-to-ceiling window. She pushed her nose to the glass and stared out at the city and the thousands of lights blinking on in the surrounding buildings as twilight fell. She seemed mesmerized by the view and would no doubt leave a dozen tiny handprints for the janitorial crew.

Kelly checked out the rest of the reception area. There was a large desk to one side of the high-ceilinged space where Angel was peering into a silver compact while smearing coal-black gloss on her lips, a dramatic contrast to her pale skin. Angel waved a few fingers at them without taking her eyes from the mirror. Kelly smiled back.

The rest of the room was furnished like a large living area with comfortable couches and chairs in shades of brown and turquoise, small wooden tables in a dark finish and huge pottery urns. The walls were a pristine white, but the floor was richly hued terra-cotta tile in Native American fashion that complemented the pictures and decorative items in the high-ceilinged room. The result was a look that—unlike Angel—seemed very welcoming.

"Cool," Angel announced, giving Kelly the once-over now that she'd finished her grooming chores. "You look just like you did on TV. I always liked you, but never understood why you let that jerk husband of yours push you around? What was his name? Brad, wasn't it?"

"Oh, you're talking about my husband on the soap."

"Sure. Who else?"

"Kelly, this is Angel," Jack said. He turned to Angel. "Sounds as if I don't have to tell you who Kelly is, but the delightful young lady at the window is Alex."

Kelly extended a hand. "Nice to meet you, Angel."

"Yeah, I'm sorry about…" Angel glanced toward Alex as her voice dropped to a low whisper. "Your real husband, you know. I'm sorry."

"Thanks." So Angel knew that Kelly had yet to tell Alex her father had been murdered. She guessed that meant all of PPS had heard and she couldn't help but wonder what else they knew about her.

Alex left the window and walked over to stand

beside them. She looked up at Angel quizzically, then fit her hand into Kelly's. "Is she a witch?"

"No, of course not. I'm sorry, Angel. I'm sure Alex didn't mean that the way it sounded."

"It's okay," Angel said. "It's probably just the black dress."

Black dress, black shoes, black lipstick, black nail polish and more bling jangling from her multiple piercings than a heavy metal band.

Angel dropped her compact and gloss into her top desk drawer. "Lenny's already been up here looking for you, Jack. He said to send you his way the minute you got here."

"Thanks. Do you know if Sara's around? I'd like to see if she can watch Alex for a few minutes."

"She's out, but I'll watch the kid, as long as you don't take all night. I'm off duty at six, you know, and unlike the rest of you, I've got a life."

"I don't think Alex would—"

"Want me to paint your nails?" Angel asked before Kelly could finish her protest. "I can paint a scorpion on your thumbnail. They're really gory. That's like cool, you know."

"What's a scorpion?"

"Kind of like a spider with a long stinger. But I can paint other stuff, too, like bats and such."

Alex left Kelly's side and sidled up next to Angel. "I want a spider."

Kelly quit worrying that Alex wouldn't take to Angel and started worrying that she would. But she had more pressing issues to consider, and she could sense a steadily growing tenseness in Jack that added to her unease.

Her heels clicked noisily as they hurried down the well-lit hallway and past a number of closed doors. "Are all of those offices?"

"A few are offices. The rest are conference rooms, databases, a lounge, your typical headquarters stuff. We have a kitchen, too, where you can usually rummage around and find a snack if you get hungry while working in the middle of the night. And there're a couple of camping spaces for emergencies."

"Is camping space some protection lingo we laymen don't understand?"

"It's a room with a bed in it, so you can camp out if you get too tired to drive home, or if you just need to catch a little shut-eye and go right back to work."

"Where's your office?"

"I don't exactly have an office. I'm not senior enough for that. I have a cubicle in the northeast work area, near the tech guys. Makes it easier to run over and interfere with them every time I have a question."

"They must love that."

"This is it." Jack stopped at a closed door and once again peered into a rectangular box, waiting a second until the door slid open. "Extra precaution due to the costly equipment and the nature of the work that goes on in this area," Jack explained as he ushered her inside.

The walls were lined with cubicles, each about six-by-eight. The ones in her view contained a desk, overhead shelves and state-of-the-art computer monitors. There were at least a half-dozen men in the first row of cubicles, some at their computers, one staring into space and a couple talking on the phone.

Jack spoke to everyone they passed, but didn't stop or bother introducing her to anyone until they reached the end of the row and a heavily freckled guy with bright red hair that stuck out in all directions like porcupine quills.

"Hold it one sec," the guy said without looking up. "Need a megaminute to copy and save these files. Uh-huh, uh-huh, uh-huh. Got 'em." The guy finally lifted his fingers and swiveled his chair around so that he faced them. "I was on a hot streak."

"Did it concern Nick Warner?" Jack asked.

"You guessed it."

"This is Nick's wife."

The lanky redhead stood and extended a hand. "I'm Lenny. Sorry."

She wasn't sure if he meant he was sorry about Nick's death or sorry she'd been his wife. Or maybe sorry that he was Lenny. But she liked his smile and his freckles and was thankful he didn't have black gloss on his lips or studs in his nose.

Lenny went back to his keyboard. "I hate to be the harbinger of bad tidings, Mrs. Warner, but in case you don't already know it, your late husband was up to his neck in debt."

"You can call me Kelly, and exactly how much debt are we talking about?"

"Looks to be about eight mil." Lenny hit a few keys and a new screen popped up on his monitor. "Take a look at his credit report."

She did, and there it was. A long list of names, all of them creditors, and Lenny was still scrolling past more. She didn't see a total sum on the report, but she could easily see how the figures could add up to eight million dollars."

"How could that happen?" she asked.

"The more you make, the more they'll finance for you." Jack pulled her up a chair so that she could sit and still have a good view of the monitor.

She skimmed the list of creditors. There had to be at least a million dollars in credit card debt alone. Three million still owed on the yacht he'd bought two years ago to salve his wounded spirit after his last movie bombed. The Porsche, Lamborghini, and Mercedes all had huge outstanding balances—and he'd purchased a two-hundred-and-eighty-thousand dollar Aston Martin two months ago that she'd never even seen, much less driven.

She took a closer look at the information. "It looks as if he only pays the minimum on every account and pays that late."

"There's more," Lenny said.

"Surely not more bills."

"Your house in Beverly Hills is mortgaged to the hilt."

She muttered a curse under her breath. Nick had never told her any of this, and she was sure Mitchell didn't know about it, either. He'd have read Nick the riot act long before now. "Who's responsible for his debts if there's no money left in his estate?"

"That's the really bad news, Kelly. It looks as if your name's on a lot of the accounts."

"I never cosigned for anything."

"Then someone signed for you."

"How much are we talking about?"

"Approximately half of the total."

"That's four million dollars. All I have is some money I saved from when I was acting. It's not nearly enough to cover that."

"The estate will have the income from *Savage Thunder*," Jack said. "That should cover the debt."

"Unless it bombs like the last two. Nick's already received his up-front money. Any additional payments are based on box office receipts."

"Did he have a life insurance policy?"

"I doubt it, but if he did, you can bet my name won't be on it."

She leaned against the cubicle. "Is this why you had me come in? If so, I think your investigation sucks."

"Look at the figures again," Jack said. "Those expenditures look outrageous at first glance, but they're not that out of line with what other people in Nick's income bracket spend."

"Then why the debt?" Kelly asked.

"I don't know," Jack admitted, "but when we find

out, I think we'll know what got Nick killed and why your name is on someone's hit list."

"But I've never been involved in Nick's finances. I used the credit cards he gave me, but I assumed he was paying them off every month. If he was into anything illegal or risky, he never shared that with me, so why would anyone think they had to get rid of me?"

Lenny started typing again. "Let's go back to the facts. One, an intruder breaks into the house in the wee hours of Friday morning, runs into Kelly but doesn't try to harm her. Two, less than twelve hours later, someone aims an assault rifle at her and tries to blow her to kingdom come. If we assume those two incidents are connected, then what happened in between them that changed the scope of the danger?"

"And the obvious answer," Jack said, "is that her husband was murdered by an unsub."

Kelly raised a hand as if she were in class. "Talk English, please. What's an unsub?"

"Unknown subject," Lenny answered.

"Aren't both of you overlooking the fact that Detective Carter has arrested a suspect."

"Bates didn't do it." Jack and Lenny made the pronouncement at the exact same time.

"How can you be so sure?" she countered. "The man confessed to the crime."

"I ran a full background check on David Bates," Lenny said. "He's been in and out of so many mental institutions he has his own skeleton key."

"Now that's hyperbole," she said.

"Not by much. Last year the guy managed to get on the speaker system at Coors Field and insisted he'd been sent from Babe Ruth to warn about the evils of performance-enhancing drugs. Two years ago he was arrested at a Broncos game for streaking through the stands during the national anthem. He's not a killer. He's just an attention-craving psycho."

Jack straddled his chair and raked his fingers through his hair. "Back to our issue. Nick was shot, but he didn't die immediately because for some unknown reason the killer shot him in the stomach instead of the head or heart. That's not the work of a professional like we were dealing with today on the way to the airport."

"Maybe Nick saw him and tried to wrestle the gun away from him."

"So why didn't the unsub finish him off after he put three bullets in him?"

"It was on the street in the middle of the night. Someone was coming and our unsub had to clear out before he got caught."

"So had the unsub followed Nick all night waiting for that opportunity?"

"Or had he been partying with Nick and decided to kill him because of something that happened that evening?"

"And how are Friday night's break-in, Nick's murder and the sniper fire today related?"

Kelly's head swam as she tried to keep up with the comments and questions that Lenny and Jack shot off like a pack of firecrackers on one short fuse.

Lenny took his fingers from the keyboard, leaned back and clasped his hands behind his head. "The killer didn't finish the job, so Nick ended up at the hospital instead of the morgue. Maybe he thinks Nick came to long enough to tell Kelly who shot him."

"Which she would have immediately told the police," Jack said.

Lenny turned to Kelly. "Did Nick say anything at all while you were with him at the hospital?"

She tried to think, but her memories of last night were foggy. She'd still been in shock at that point. "He groaned a few times. He tried to say something about a list. And he started to spell something, the way he used to do when he didn't want Alex to know what he was saying. He may have thought she was with me."

"What were the letters?" Lenny asked.

"*T-L-N. T-M-L.*" She shook her head. "I can't remember."

"TCM," Jack said.

"*T-C-M,*" Lenny repeated the letters as he typed them. "I don't think there's a word in the English language that starts with *tcm.*"

"Could be an acronym," Kelly said, but Lenny was already ahead of her. He'd pulled up the TCM listings from whatever search engine he was using.

"Technical Counsel of Macken Industries. Turner Classic Movies. Turnbow Construction Movers. TCM Driving Academy. The list goes on and on."

Kelly glanced at her watch. "I should go relieve Angel of Alex or at least check on her."

"Let me do it," Jack volunteered. "You stay here and give Lenny any additional information he needs to keep his search progressing."

"I don't know what else I can tell him. He seems to know more about Nick than I do."

"Where did Nick grow up?" Lenny asked.

"Don't tell me we have to go back that far. We'll be here all night."

"You'll be out of here in forty-five minutes, an hour, tops. Town and state."

She took a deep breath and exhaled slowly. She had her doubts any of this would lead to Nick's killer or her sharpshooter, but she didn't have any better ideas. "He grew up in Joliet, Illinois, but I think he was actually born in Wisconsin."

"Yep. Madison."

"If you already know all of this, what's the point of the questions?"

"Ever look for a needle in a haystack?"

"No."

"Me, either," Lenny admitted, "but I figure if there's one there and you poke your hand between enough blades of hay, you'll eventually find it. I'm poking now, looking for discrepancies as well as facts. If I feed Jack enough info, he'll figure it all out. You'll think he's getting nowhere. Then all of a sudden, pow! He'll have all the answers. He's the master. Now, names of ten of Nick's best friends."

Kelly was certain this was going to be one of the longest hours of her life.

Saturday, 9:30 p.m.
Single S Ranch

JACK THREW ANOTHER LOG on the fire and propped his foot on the hearth near where Kelly's fancy boots sat drying next to his. The ranch house had an entirely different feel with her in it. The faint fragrance of her perfume penetrated every room. The radio was tuned to an easy listening station that played the kind of ballads that struck right at the heart.

Worst of all, he could hear the water running in the bathroom and the thought of her standing naked under the shower, her body sleek with soap, had him so worked up he couldn't think straight.

He should have been over her years ago. There wasn't that much to get over, just two eighteen-year-olds giving in to raging hormones. But then she'd been the only good thing in his life of horrors.

Jack dropped to the couch and let his mind go somewhere he'd left behind years ago. The loud arguments. Coming home to find his mother passed out from tranquilizer overdoses.

And finally, the rainy night Jack's father drove his big rig off an overpass. The highway patrolman who'd investigated the accident said it was caused by the weather. Jack figured his dad just couldn't take it anymore.

He and his mother had moved to the Lake Tahoe area and into her parents' small lake house. His grandparents were no better at dealing with their daughter's addiction and unstable personality than her husband had been, and they didn't like having her or Jack around to complicate their quiet life.

Jack had begged his older sister to let him live with her in Chicago. She refused, so he spent his senior year skipping classes, roaring around the area on his Harley and getting into fights with the local jocks.

By May, he was just hanging on until the day he left for boot camp. At least that had been the situation until he'd run into some of his classmates at the lake. Kelly O'Conner, the minister's daughter, more out of than in her sky-blue bikini, had started flirting with him. And that's when his real trouble had begun.

Jack stirred the fire again, then sank to the sofa just as Kelly joined him in the den. She'd made a turban for her wet hair from one of his green towels, and she'd slipped into a pink robe that looked as if it might melt if touched.

"Nice," she said. "I love a fire when it's snowing. It's one of the things I miss living in Beverly Hills." She pulled off the turban and tossed her head so that her wet hair swung freely in front of the fire screen.

"I tried to call Mitchell and ask what he knew about Nick's debts," she said. "He didn't answer his cell phone or the one in his hotel room. I left him a message." She straightened and let her hair fall down around her shoulders. "Do you have any wine? I think a small glass might help me sleep."

It would take a lot more than that for him. "I'm not

much of a connoisseur, but there are a couple of bottles in the cupboard. Only red, I think, probably a cabernet."

"Cab would be nice. Will you have some with me?"

"Sure. Never make a lady drink alone. That's the rule, isn't it?"

"As I remember it, you were never one to follow rules."

At least she remembered something about him. He went to the kitchen, uncorked the wine and grabbed his finest crystal water glasses from the discount store in town. He worried that she'd hate the wine. It would be a lot less expensive than what she was used to.

So get off it, Jack Sanders. She's used to marriage to a gay guy. Surely you can top that.

When he returned to the den, Kelly had settled on the sofa and curled her legs beneath her robe. She looked like a cup of sherbet, light and frothy and delicious. He swallowed a string of curses, aimed at himself for thinking like some lovesick geek who'd never been alone with a woman. Even as an ignorant teenager, he'd handled things better than this.

He set the glasses on the table and poured. "I brought the bottle in here with me. You may need a refill after the last two days."

"I may, but I really don't want to talk about Nick, or the black-car shooter or my recently inherited debt. I'm overwhelmed and not even sure I've actually accepted yet that Nick's dead. Maybe that's why I can't get up the courage to talk to Alex about it."

"We can just drink and not talk at all."

"No, I want to talk, just not about unpleasant things. I know I have to deal with all of this, but I just can't face any more tonight."

"You start," he said. "I'll jump in."

She sipped her wine and stared into the fire, staying quiet so long he thought she'd changed her mind about conversation. He'd gotten his hopes up too soon.

"How did you come to settle in Denver?"

He stretched his legs in front of him and propped his feet on the coffee table so that he didn't have to face her and have his mind drift to places it shouldn't go.

"I'd decided to leave the army and was going bonkers recuperating and trying to decide what to do next with my life. Out of the blue I got a call from Cameron Morgan. He and I had met while he was with the Army Rangers, but he'd already left the military and signed on with PPS. To make a long story a little less long, he asked me to come up and look over PPS operations. I did. They offered me a job, and the rest is history."

"Do you miss the work you were doing in the army?"

"I never look back. It gets you nowhere." At least that had been his policy before Kelly had dropped back into his life.

"And I continually look back," she said, "but maybe that's because I'm not where I'd like to be in the present." She swirled the wine and watched it settle. "Were you ever married?"

"No."

"That's a short answer."

"It was a short question."

"Why not?"

He stood and walked to the fire, picked up the poker and nudged the logs until sparks shot up the chimney. "Guess I never met the right woman."

"You're smarter than me. I obviously didn't wait for the right man."

She stared into the fire, and they sat in silence until she'd finished most of her second glass of wine. "I'm incredibly tired. If you'll excuse me, Jack, I think I'll carry my glass to the sink and turn in."

"Conversation from me and cheap wine. Puts the women to sleep every time. But just leave the glass here. I'll get it."

Her lips parted in a tentative smile that didn't reach her eyes. She started to the bedroom she was sharing with Alex, but stopped and leaned against the door frame. "Thanks for taking us in. As exhausted as I am, I'm sure I'd be afraid to close my eyes anywhere else. I'd fear something would happen to Alex."

And with that she disappeared into the bedroom one door down from his. He stood in front of the fire and watched a stray ember dance its way up the chimney. Yep. The house was definitely different with her in it.

And it would be heartbreakingly empty when she left.

Sunday, 12:36 a.m.
Single S Ranch

JACK HAD JUST TURNED off the lamp when his phone vibrated and clattered against his bedside table. He checked the ID. Gilly Carter. Jack's adrenaline shot up. The detective wouldn't call this time of the night without good reason. He took the call. "What's up, Carter?"

"Sorry to bother you this late, but there are some new developments I think you and Kelly should know about."

"Do you have a new suspect in Nick's murder?"

"No, but the evidence on David Bates is pretty much down the toilet. He was nowhere near the crime scene last night. I don't even see a reason to charge him with interfering with the investigation. A half-decent attorney would get him off on mental instability, and Denver's full of half-decent attorneys."

"Then I'm guessing Bates is not why you called."

"No. We had another actor die tonight."

"Murder?"

"We haven't totally ruled it out, but there's no indication of foul play. The guy was at a party in the same hotel where the Warners were staying. He was drinking heavily and said he was going up to his room to turn in. Not fifteen minutes later, he fell from his tenth-floor balcony."

Nick let out a low whistle. "That had to make a mess. Anybody I know?"

"Hal Hayden. I hear he was a good friend of Nick Warner's. I'm hoping to learn more about him from Kelly. How's she holding up?"

"She's having a hard time, but she's hanging in there. Her daughter's safety is her main concern at this point."

"I need her to come in tomorrow."

"You can ask her about Hal Hayden on the phone."

"It's a little more serious than that. Let's just say she's a person of interest, and we need to talk."

"You know damn well she didn't have anything to do with her husband's death."

"I agree it's not likely, considering that an attempt was made on her life, but I've got a police chief who's ready to chop heads if we don't come up with a viable suspect and a motive for the murder. He likes to hear that I've left no stone unturned. So what time do you want to bring Kelly in to see me?"

"Snow's coming down pretty good out here. Roads may be impassable by morning."

"Then let's make it noon, give the plows plenty of time to do their work."

"Noon it is, but it's a waste of your time and ours, Carter. Believe me, Kelly doesn't have a clue what her late husband was into."

"I hope you're right."

He was right. Jack no longer had any doubts in that department, but Hal's death added a whole new level of complications to an investigation he still didn't have a handle on.

If Hal Hayden had help plunging to his death, it would be the third attack in less than forty-eight hours, all of them with some connection to Nick Warner.

And unless Jack was way off base, there was a bullet with Kelly's name on it already in a chamber and waiting to be fired. He planned to make damn sure it never reached its mark.

Chapter Eight

Kelly slipped on the icy terrain, the mountain growing steeper, and the blinding snow and howling wind making every step a battle.

Faster, Kelly. Faster. Nick urged her on as the sounds of gunfire exploded around her. And then she looked behind her, and there was Nick, laughing and aiming an AK-47 at her heart.

Kelly jerked awake, knowing it was a nightmare yet still clasping the sheet so tightly that sharp pains needled her fingers. The cold from the dream had settled in her chest like sheets of ice, and her arms and legs felt as if she'd been running for miles.

She blinked and rubbed her eyes, then looked to the bed next to her to check on Alex. The covers were shoved back, but Alex wasn't tangled in them the way had Kelly expected she'd be.

A quick burst of intermingled giggling and barking relieved her mind. She took a deep breath and her nostrils filled with the invigorating odors of frying bacon and coffee. She felt around on the night table looking for her watch, and then finally found it on the floor. Apparently she'd done some serious arm-swinging during her restless sleep.

She groaned when she saw the time. She hadn't meant to sleep this late. Seduced by the waiting coffee, she made quick work of wiggling into a pair of comfortable jeans and a mauve sweater. She splashed her face with cold water, brushed her teeth, pushed her hair behind her ears and decided that would do. Not paparazzi-ready, but…

The days of worrying about that were coming to a close. Nick was dead. The reality of it hit more solidly at that instant than it had any time since she'd left the hospital.

She perched on the edge of the old claw-foot tub while the knowledge took root. Nick had been her husband—yet they were practically strangers. She hadn't hated him, nor had she actually liked him, though this was the first time she'd ever let herself admit that. Perhaps it was learning of his tremendous debt that made the truth clearer.

He had to be the *star* in all aspects of his life, no matter the cost.

Everyone always raved about his generosity, but

even that was about him. He liked the attention he garnered from giving expensive gifts, throwing wild parties and taking his friends on fabulous trips. Liked having his wife shop in the most elite boutiques and wear designer gowns whenever he needed her on his arm to quell the growing rumors.

Nick the magnificent. A magazine had once used that as the title of an article about him, and he'd had the page blown up and framed. It hung over the pool table in his massive den.

But he was dead now, and Kelly wouldn't concentrate on his faults. He'd loved Alex, and that was the legacy she'd pass on to her daughter.

Kelly found Alex in the middle of the kitchen floor, still in her pajamas, tussling and sharing kisses with the collie. "I beated you up, Mommy," she announced. "But I didn't beated Jack up. Cowboys get up early, huh, Jack?"

"Can't have slackers on the ranch."

"And Jack let Stormy come inside and play with me cause it's too cold for me to go outside and play with him. Pete and Repeat didn't want to come inside. They were chasing rabbits."

Kelly stooped and gave her daughter a kiss on the cheek. "I'm glad Stormy came in to play."

"He sleeps in the barn with the other dogs, cause they're his friends. Friends can sleep together, huh, Jack?"

"Friends have been know to do that."

He poured a cup of coffee and handed it to Kelly.

"There's sweetener in the blue canister right behind you. I don't have any of that powdered cream."

"I can use milk." She opened the refrigerator and poured straight from the carton they'd had delivered with the rest of the groceries last evening. "Can I help with the cooking?"

Jack turned a slice of bacon, then jumped back to keep from getting splattered from a spray of hot grease. "I've got it under control. Alex and I have already eaten."

"So why are you still frying bacon?"

"For you. I was going to give you five more minutes of sleep before I woke you. Luckily, you saved me the trouble."

"Good. I don't want to be known as a slacker. Guess I should have mentioned that I don't normally eat breakfast."

"No wonder you stay so thin. Probably have a personal trainer, as well."

"As a matter of fact, I do." Make that did.

"You California babes do suffer. But you'll hurt my feelings if you don't at least try my pancakes." He poured a ladle of batter onto the sputtering griddle.

"Your coffee's divine, I'll give you that."

She took another long sip, savoring the taste and the warmth. She tried to remember the last time she'd sat in a kitchen with a man while he cooked breakfast. It had definitely been before Nick. They hadn't had meals together in a couple of years, and even when they had, the cooking had been done by a chef.

Kelly finished her coffee, then refilled the mug as Jack set a plate of fluffy pancakes and crispy bacon in front of her. She poured a tiny river of maple syrup in the center of the short stack and watched it dribble to the edges before cutting off a bite with her fork and slipping it between her lips.

"Hmm. Wow! Good."

"I told you."

He hadn't lied, and with the first bite she realized that she was famished. Jack kept her company while she ate, but the talk stayed light with no mention of Nick's debts or yesterday's attack, since Alex and Stormy were still in the middle of the kitchen floor.

"That's it," she said, when she was down to the last half of the last pancake. "I can't eat another bite." She got up to dump the remains down the garbage disposal and rinse her plate. Jack walked over to Alex. "How would you like to watch some TV?"

She jumped up and started singing and dancing around Stormy. "Can I watch cartoons?"

"I'll see what I can do."

Alex followed at Jack's heels and the collie at hers. Kelly stayed behind, knowing that luring Alex to the den was the signal that it was time to forget laid-back congeniality and get down to business. Jack mixed the two almost seamlessly. Maybe that's why the lines between old friend and client kept getting entangled in her mind.

Only they'd never really been friends. They'd gone from acquaintances to unbridled passion to strangers in less time than it took most couples to orchestrate the first kiss. She wondered if even Lenny would have been fast enough to track that progression.

Jack reentered the kitchen alone, the TV blaring loudly behind him.

He took the seat opposite hers. "We need to talk."

"I know. I left my phone in the bedroom. I should get it and call Mitchell again. I'm certain he doesn't know about the debt. He'd have made Nick cut back on his spending."

"Did he have that kind of clout with Nick?"

"Absolutely. Nick knew he owed his career to Mitchell. He'd managed him from day one." She stood to go for her phone.

"The call can wait."

"Okay." She sat back down. "Why do I think you have bad news?"

"Maybe you're psychic." He leaned forward and toyed with a fork that had been left on the table. "Detective Carter called last night after you went to bed, actually a few hours after you went to bed."

"What did he want at that time of the night?"

"Hal Hayden fell from the balcony of his hotel room. He was ten floors up."

"Oh, no." The image made her ill, and sorry she'd eaten. "How did that happen?"

"The investigation isn't complete, but there was

no obvious sign of foul play. He was drunk, so he could have just fallen."

"First Nick and now Hal. How bizarre—and tragic."

"Detective Carter said they were friends. Were they more?"

She hesitated, but there was no reason to deny the truth. "Yes, they were more than friends."

"You know that for a fact?"

She nodded. "I told you that I caught Nick in a compromising position."

"And that was with Hal?"

"Yes, six months ago, and I still see Hal in and out of the house on a regular basis. In fact he always seems to be around. Do you think he could have been distraught enough over Nick's death to kill himself?"

Jack pushed the fork aside. "Do you?"

"I don't know. I always figured he just liked the lifestyle Nick afforded him—though now we know Nick couldn't afford it."

"Always fun to be with the king."

"Yeah," she sighed. "Then again, he might have been crazy about Nick. My husband had a way of making you believe that things were all about you when they were really all about him." She'd been naive enough to fall for that once.

She felt guilty for thinking about that now. Guilt on top of everything else. This was all so hard.

"The detective called for another reason, too. He wants you to come in for questioning."

She had her second sinking sensation of the conversation. "What do you mean by questioning?"

"He'll probably ask about your relationship with Nick."

"He can't think I'm a suspect. I was with you when Nick was shot, and I surely didn't try to kill myself yesterday."

"He knows all of that. The questioning is likely routine."

"Did he refer to me as a suspect?"

"He referred to you as a person of interest. He's looking for a motive."

"A motive?"

"He may have heard that you were planning to divorce Nick."

Kelly exploded. "Divorce is a long way from—" She stopped midtirade. She had to calm down before Alex heard her and came running in to see what was wrong. But the frustration kept eating away at her. "I'm not involved, Jack."

"You're preaching to the choir, but there's no getting around seeing Carter. Either you go in willingly or he'll get a warrant. I told him we'll be there at noon."

"*We?* You throw that out so casually. This is about *me,* Jack. *I'm* the person of interest."

"You can refuse to answer questions until you have a lawyer present."

"I'm not bringing in an attorney. I have nothing to hide. For God's sake, I was almost a victim myself. The monsters could have killed Alex—and you.

Carter can't just disregard that. You were a witness, and the car we were in is riddled with bullets from an assault rifle. And besides I can't go running into his office. I have Alex."

"We can take her back to headquarters. I'll call Evangeline. She'll assign someone to watch her. It's all part of the package when you sign on with PPS."

"It seems as if you and Carter have this all worked out." The comment wasn't fair and she knew it, but she was facing enough without the police working against her. The mountain from her nightmare had become real, and she was sliding down it and into a chasm that was growing deeper by the second.

Sunday, 11:08 a.m.
Downtown Denver

THE SNOW HAD STOPPED falling, and the sun peeked from behind a layer of gray clouds as they entered Denver's downtown area. Jack had been silent for most of the drive into town which was fine with Kelly. She was tired of talking about things she seemed powerless to change.

Her cell phone rang. "It's Mitchell," she said, checking the caller ID. "What do I tell him?"

"Just say you need to see him this afternoon. Best not to get into the debt issue over the phone."

"Hi, Mitchell, where have you been? I've been trying to reach you since yesterday."

"I changed hotels. Didn't they tell you?"

"No, but I also tried your cell phone. It's constantly busy."

"I know. Nick's murder has created a media storm. I've been so upset I can barely deal with the situation. You know how I felt about Nick. He was like a brother. And now there's Hal Hayden. Did you hear?"

"I heard."

"This will be known as the Film Festival from hell. Well, back to the reason I called, I just talked to the medical examiner. He's released Nick's body. I need to know where it should be delivered."

"The Beverly Hills Funeral Home. I called them yesterday and they'll take care of everything including a private service in their chapel." Very private. In fact she might not even make it back in time to attend, not unless she was certain there was no risk to Alex.

"I hate to badger you about this, Kelly, but have you booked a flight home?"

"Not yet."

"I know you're concerned about yours and Alex's safety. So am I, so I took the liberty of calling the company that installed your home security. They're going to check out everything and make sure the alarm system is working properly."

"I appreciate that."

"And I've contacted a bodyguard service in Beverly Hills. They've assured me they can guarantee your protection, though I really don't think you have a thing to worry about. That attack on the high-

way was most likely a case of mistaken identity—
or else Jack Sanders was the target."

"I guess that's a possibility."

"If that's it, I should get back to the media feeding frenzy."

"That's not quite it. I really need to talk to you
in person."

"Certainly. Why don't you stop by my hotel
sometime after three? I'm tied up until then."

"I'd like you to meet with both Jack and me at
PPS Headquarters."

The silent pause was so long that she feared she'd
lost the connection.

"I have no interest in meeting with Jack."

"It's important, Mitchell. I've learned some things
about Nick's finances that are very troubling. I need
to find out what you know of the situation, and the
data I need to discuss it intelligently is at PPS."

"I see. In that case, I guess I have no choice."

"Can you make it for three?"

"I'll try. I may be a few minutes late."

"Good. Hold on and Jack can give you directions."

Jack turned into the parking garage entrance of
PPS and swiped his card at the security control
before putting her phone to his ear.

A minute later Kelly was holding Alex's hand
and walking across the well-lit garage to the private
elevator that led directly to the top floor and the
entrance to PPS. She was still in her jeans and

wearing sensible, low-heeled boots, a canvas tote slung over her shoulders.

Strange how the priorities in her life had changed over the last sixty hours. Fashion and keeping up appearances meant nothing. Now it was all about staying alive.

THE YOUNG WOMAN behind the reception desk today bore little resemblance to Angel. Her skirt was brown, her shirt was a nice shade of lavender, and her stylish blazer was a muted plaid. More striking differences were the absence of chunky, dangling silver from her ears and gauche studs in her nose and lips.

"Where's Angel?" Alex asked, obviously displeased that her new friend wasn't there to greet her.

"It's Angel's day off," Jack said. He introduced them to Elisha. The attractive brunette was both soft-spoken and businesslike.

"Mrs. Prescott asked that you stop by her office. Shall I tell her you're on your way?"

"Sure thing. What about Lenny? Is he in his cube?"

"I think so. I know he's in the area."

"Then I'm sure I can find him."

"Angel painted a spider on my fingernail," Alex said, holding up her thumb for Elisha's admiration.

"That's nice," Elisha said, then went back to whatever she'd been typing into her computer.

"It's Sunday," Kelly said as they took the hallway in the opposite direction from the way they'd gone yesterday. "Don't PPS employees ever take a day off?"

"Sure, just no particular day. If you're on an assignment you work the days and hours it requires to get the job done right."

"But the tech guys must work regular hours."

"There're always a few on duty, and I've yet to be here at any time of the night when there weren't at least a couple of agents in the office. Danger doesn't watch the clock."

Alex danced in front of them, letting her fingers trail along the white walls and occasionally stopping to peek through an open doorway. High tech meant nothing to her. PPS was just another playground.

"Evangeline must be quite a woman to keep a place like this going. What is her background?"

"She's a former FBI agent and her husband, Robert, was an undercover agent with M16 before he came to the U.S."

"What's M16?"

"Great Britain's Secret Intelligence Service. M16 is their external division, handling espionage outside the UK."

"That explains the sophisticated equipment and the heavy emphasis on investigation. What did you mean yesterday when you said Angel was one of Evangeline's projects?"

Evangeline adopts people, or I guess it's more like she rescues them. I didn't get the story firsthand, but word is that she was raised in a foster home and she'll go the extra mile to help out people who might have experienced the same kind of misfortune."

"I like her already."

"Everybody does. That's her standing by the door to the corner office."

Alex made a beeline toward Evangeline and was excitedly showing her the gory work of art on her fingernail by the time Kelly and Jack caught up.

Jack made the introductions, and Kelly was duly impressed. Evangeline looked positively regal in a pair of gray slacks and a cashmere sweater the shade of buttercups.

"I've looked forward to meeting you," Evangeline said, as Kelly and Jack took a seat. "It's a little-known fact around here, but I used to escape to my office at least once a week to watch the soap you were on while I ate lunch. Your character was one of my favorites. You wore such beautiful clothes."

"We had a terrific wardrobe lady." Kelly was glad Evangeline hadn't said it was her acting that she'd loved. The statement would have killed her credibility.

Evangeline reached into her desk drawer, pulled out a box of washable markers and a drawing pad and set them on the edge of her desk.

Alex eyed them immediately and sauntered over. "I like to draw."

"Would you like to use my markers?"

"Yes, ma'am." Alex smiled sheepishly at Evangeline. "I like red."

"Me, too," Evangeline agreed.

Alex took the markers from the desk. "I'll draw you a red picture."

"I'd like that. Here, take the pad and you can draw lots of pictures."

"I brought some other things to keep her busy, too," Kelly said. She patted the tote bag she'd set down beside her chair. "There are a couple of DVDs, some books, some games, and her Pooh bear. When she gets tired, she likes to cuddle with him. And there's a peanut butter and jelly sandwich in there for her lunch and some grapes and cookies if she wants a snack. I didn't bring milk. Jack said there was always milk in the PPS refrigerator."

"Always," Evangeline said. "There might even be peanut butter in the kitchen. Occasionally an agent won't go home for dinner for days."

"I don't know if Lenny has a home," Jack joked. "I think he's taken over one of the campsites."

"We'll kick him out today and make room for Alex if she needs a nap."

"I don't take naps," Alex said.

"Then we won't worry about that. You can draw pictures, watch videos and play with Sara. She stayed with you in the hotel. Do you remember her?"

"Uh-huh. She's fun."

"She thinks you're pretty fun, too. Jack, why don't you take Alex to Harry Gayfer's office? Sara's confiscated it for the afternoon so that Alex will be more comfortable."

"I'll draw her a picture," Alex said. "And Mommy one, too. But not you, Jack. You have a fish."

Kelly hugged her daughter and gave her a parting

kiss on the cheek. "Be good, sweetheart. I'll be back to get you soon."

Kelly knew this was a setup for her to be alone with Evangeline. She figured she'd know why by the time Jack got back.

Evangeline settled in the leather chair behind her desk. "I'm sorry about your husband, Kelly. No matter what kind of relationship you had, I know this is difficult for you."

Kelly wondered if everyone at PPS knew about her and Nick's relationship. "You're right, it is difficult, and doubly so since the danger has extended to my daughter."

"And to you. Jack said you had a very close call on the way to the airport."

"If Jack hadn't been driving, we'd almost certainly be dead."

"Jack is one PPS's most experienced and knowledgeable agents. He's not one to sing his own praises, but under the circumstances I thought knowing his capabilities would give you added reassurance and hopefully relieve your mind a bit."

So that's why Evangeline had made a point of talking to her without Jack present. "Thanks, I do have confidence in Jack, but I'm not sure how long I'll be able to stay in Denver."

"Jack's convinced that the ranch is the safest place for you and Alex right now. I must say I agree."

"It's not the safety of the ranch that concerns me. I'm eager to return home because I haven't told Alex about her father's death yet. It seems cruel to give her that kind of news when she has nothing familiar around her to cushion the blow."

"She has you, Kelly, and I'd be willing to bet you're the most important constant in her world. When it's time to tell her, I'm sure you'll do it well."

"I wish I were that confident. I've made a lot of mistakes in the past and most of them have come back to haunt me." Kelly glanced to the window and the spectacular view of the city and the mountains beyond. "I don't know why I'm telling you this."

"Sometimes it helps to talk, especially when you've been hit with so much at once."

"And it just keeps coming."

"Jack says that you're a smart woman and a super mother, Kelly. You'll come through this just fine. So will Alex. Trust Jack and PPS with your safety and trust your own instincts with everything else."

Their conversation was interrupted by Jack's return and the urgency in his voice when he reminded her that they needed to see Lenny before they left for their meeting with Detective Carter.

Evangeline walked them to the door. "I've assigned Lenny to work with you full-time until this is resolved, Jack."

"Thanks. I've got a hunch I'll need him."

"Keep me posted."

"You got it."

Jack started down the hall, but Kelly lingered. "It was a real pleasure meeting you and thanks for the pep talk." She extended her hand, but Evangeline pulled her into a quick but warm hug instead.

"Good luck, Kelly. I have every confidence this will all work out. You and Jack make a great team."

Her and Jack a team? An interesting concept, but not one she had time to think about now.

She hurried to catch up with Jack. She was still nervous about the meeting with Detective Carter, but she felt better about the general situation. At least she did until they reached Lenny's cubicle.

"Good news and bad," he said before they'd even said hello. "Which do you want first?"

"The good," Kelly answered.

"I think I know which TCM Nick was referring to."

"And the bad?" Jack asked.

"The TCM Nick was referring to."

Chapter Nine

Lenny tapped a few keys and pulled up the home page of Tri Corp. Media. "Are either of you familiar with this company?"

"I am," Kelly said. "In fact the wife of the head of the company is in Denver this week for the film festival. You saw her, Jack. Friday night. She was that woman who grabbed my arm and insisted I come to her party as you were herding me out the door of the theater."

"I remember her. Thought I might have to shoot her to get her to let go of you. So what was Nick's connection to TCM?"

"He's one of their big-time investors," Lenny said. "Really big-time, which helps explain why he doesn't have money to pay his creditors."

"How did you find that out?" Kelly asked.

"From his bank account records." Lenny pulled up a new screen, this one a spreadsheet of three bank accounts bearing Nick's name and social security number.

"Isn't it illegal to tap into someone's bank accounts?"

The redheaded technician looked at her as if she'd dropped from an alien planet. "The information's there. I'm just looking at it, not stealing his money. Not that he has much to steal. Besides, I didn't tap into his bank accounts. I tapped into his online files with his accountant firm, using information I obtained from you, by the way."

Jack leaned closer so he could see what Lenny was pulling up on the screen. "Here's a check for sixty-two thousand dollars made out to Chance for Children last week. Is that a legit organization?"

"I haven't had a chance to check it out."

"It's legitimate."

Both men stared at her. "Are you sure?" Jack asked. "I've never heard of it."

"I'm positive," she said. "I established and manage it. We choose promising students from poor families and try to give them an opportunity to succeed. We see that they have at least two healthy meals a day, decent clothes and shoes to wear, attend a summer camp and we provide tutors and some kind of private enrichment classes such as dance or music lessons." She stopped for breath. "Sorry, didn't mean to get up on my soapbox. Just the stress."

"That's nice work," Lenny said, his fingers still flying over the keys. "Lot of rich people don't care."

"But many of them do," she said, "and a good many of those contribute to our fund. Even Nick occasionally, but I never got that check."

"TCM's not the only company Nick was investing in," Lenny said, "but it got the bulk of his money."

"How much bulk are we talking about?" Jack asked.

"A million dollars last year."

Jack gave a low whistle. "That's a lot of bulk."

"Is that why you said the bad news was Tri Corp.?" Kelly asked, trying to get all this straight.

"I said that because Tri Corp. has a lot of people making huge investments."

Jack turned back to Kelly. "Which means the company is exceptionally talented at getting people to make sizable investments."

"Is that illegal?"

"Not at all," Jack said. "It's the way big business runs."

"And TCM is a growing business with their fingers in lots of pies, so there probably is money to be made there." Lenny handed Jack a printout. "Here's a list of Nick's other investments. As you can see, they were mostly in extremely speculative real estate ventures or in shady companies promising huge profits and a quick rate of return."

Kelly watched as Lenny started highlighting the checks related to Nick's investments. The amount of money involved was staggering. "Why would he keep investing money when he was sliding into financial ruin?"

"It's not that uncommon," Jack said. "It's similar to having a gambling problem. The more desperate he got for funds, the more money he'd invest in get-rich-quick schemes, hoping for the big payoff."

"But it never came," she said.

"He wasn't a complete failure at his investments," Lenny said, pulling up yet another screen. "Three weeks ago, Nick made two million dollars profit selling TCM a hundred acres he owned in Puerto Escondido. The deal was sealed in Mexico and profit from that sale never went into any of Nick's American bank accounts."

"I guess you found that out on the Internet, too."

"Some of it," Lenny said. "And I've got connections in Mexico. You know, you scratch my back, I scratch yours."

Naturally. This was PPS. "Why would TCM pay so much for the land?"

"No doubt so that they can make even more profit," Jack said. "Tourism is booming down there and they could be planning to develop a high-end resort."

"Or they could think there's enough oil and natural gas to make drilling profitable," Lenny said.

Kelly was still puzzled. "Why wouldn't Nick put

his profit into the bank to cover his bills? Two million would have gone a long way."

"Maybe he has more millions stashed in a foreign bank," Lenny said. "He could have been planning to escape his debts by faking his death and moving to some exotic island in the South Pacific. Happens more than you know."

"Not Nick. He'd never have willingly given up his life here," Kelly said. "He loved being a movie star."

Jack stood and shoved his chair out of the way. "Bottom line is that even if Nick was trying to tell Kelly the location of the money he made from his sale to TCM, we still don't know why Nick was killed or why Kelly was targeted."

"Good point," Lenny agreed.

"I want to take another look at those bank accounts later, but we need to leave now so Kelly can make her noon appointment with Carter."

"By all means," she said, with no attempt to hide her frustration. "Let's not keep the detective waiting. Maybe on top of all of this, I can get thrown in jail for killing my husband."

"Oh, I forgot," Lenny said. "There is one bit of good news. The blizzard they were forecasting for tomorrow afternoon appears to be stalled. Weatherman says it won't get here until late tomorrow night."

Good news for Lenny, maybe. Kelly was sure her blizzard had already arrived.

Sunday, 12:17 p.m.
Denver Police Station

THE MORE SATISFYING bit of good news was that Detective Carter didn't arrest Kelly the second she stepped into his small and extremely cluttered office. He didn't even take her to an intimidating interrogation room. In fact, he was very accommodating, even offering her a diet soda. He did, however, insist that they talk without Jack being present.

She and Jack had talked on the way over. He hadn't recommended she lie to Carter, but he had suggested that she only answer direct questions and that she not volunteer any of the information that Lenny had learned. He stressed that PPS had a lot better chance of identifying the danger if nothing of what Lenny had learned was leaked to the police or the media just yet.

The detective walked back into his office and handed her a cold can of soda, then dropped into the seat of power behind his desk. He wadded an empty fast-food bag and tossed it into the trash can, but left a half-eaten steak sandwich resting on a paper napkin at his right elbow.

"Did you know Hal Hayden?" he asked.

"Not well, but he was a friend of Nick's and had parts in his last two movies."

"Would you say he and Nick were close friends?"

"I don't know enough about any of Nick's friendships to classify them."

"I've heard they were extremely close."

So he knew now that Nick was gay. It hadn't taken him long to discover that. She was glad, though Mitchell wouldn't like it. The lies had gone on too long.

"That could well be," she admitted. "I know they spent a lot of time together."

"Did you confront your husband about his relationship with Hal?"

"No."

"Why not?

"Because we were a couple in name only. I planned to get a divorce right after we returned to California. That is what you want to hear, isn't it, that I was planning to divorce Nick?"

He took a deep breath and exhaled sharply. "I know it sounds as if I'm harassing you. I'm not. I just need to know everything you know about your husband's murder."

"If I knew who killed Nick, don't you think I'd have said when some lunatic with an AK-47 fired on the car I was in with my daughter?"

"Unless you thought you had good reason to keep quiet."

"I don't know what you're talking about."

"Was Nick blackmailing someone or involved in something illegal?"

"Not that I know of."

"What about Hal?"

"How would I know? He's Nick's friend, not mine. We seldom speak except to say hello in passing."

"Then how do you explain this note that was

found in Hayden's hotel room?" Carter took a plastic-encased slip of paper from a folder on his desk and handed it to her.

Her name was on the top with the names of two men beneath it. She studied the note for only a few seconds before handing it back to him. "I don't know those men, and I have no idea why my name is linked with theirs."

"Those are both violent criminals who've either served time or gotten off on one technicality or another." Carter clasped his hands together and leaned in close as if the two of them were involved in a conspiracy.

"Tell me what you know, Kelly. If you're innocent, and I believe you are, then tell me so that we can stop a killer before he comes after you again."

She threw up her hands in exasperation. "I didn't write the names. I don't know those men. I don't know why Hal had that note in his room. And I don't know who killed Nick."

"Jack Sanders may think he's invincible, Kelly, but he's not. You need the police. Don't play around with yours and your daughter's lives."

"I don't know anything to tell you. How many times do I have to say that before you believe me?"

Carter glared at her and cracked his knuckles. "I could arrest you as a suspect, you know. The betrayed wife getting even. It's classic motivation."

"You could, but we both know I didn't do it. I have an alibi and I was shot at the next day by a man wielding an assault rifle. So arresting me would only make you look desperate for a suspect."

He placed his outstretched hands flat on his desk. "And I'm not that desperate—yet. You can go, but if you want to drop Jack Sanders I can probably make a case for getting you around-the-clock police protection."

"Thanks, but I'll stick with Jack." He might not be invincible, but he makes great pancakes.

Sunday, 12:59 p.m.
In PPS Car

JACK'S CELL PHONE rang just as he and Kelly stepped into the car. He was eager to hear what Kelly had to say, but the call was from the medical examiner, and he really needed to hear the results of Nick's autopsy.

"Excuse me, Kelly, I have to take this one."

"Do you have results for me?"

"Three bullet wounds. Gilly Carter was here when I pulled them out. He said they were from a nine millimeter handgun, if that helps."

"That helps. Thanks. Did it appear the bullets were fired at close range?"

"Extremely close, and at an upward angle."

Then Nick might have been struggling to take the gun from the shooter. If he hadn't been drunk and high, he might have saved his own life.

"Did it look as if he'd been in a fight?"

"No marks on the face to indicate that. No scratches above or below the wounds. No trauma to the head. Those are the high points. Does Mrs. Warner want me to fax the full report to her at PPS?"

"Yeah, do you need her to tell you that? She's sitting right here."

"No, she put your name down on the release form at the hospital. I'll send it on over. Give her my condolences."

"Will do."

Kelly didn't wait for him to ask how her meeting with Carter went before blurting out two names.

"Devon Degrazia and Billy Sheffield. Have you heard of them?"

Unfortunately, he had. Knew them by those names and the variety of aliases they went by.

Degrazia had actually been a paid assassin for the CIA, back in the days when they had that sort of thing. Now he was in business for himself. He'd only done time for one murder and had gotten out on a technicality after spending six months in jail. He could afford the best defense attorneys.

Sheffield was small-time, in and out of jail all his life on everything from simple assault to armed robbery convictions. He was out of jail now and back on the streets in Denver. Either one would kill for pay if the situation and money were right.

Jack sped to the corner and turned just as the light turned red, then sped to the next corner and turned again, a move to lose anyone who might be tailing them.

"So have you heard of them or not?"

"I've heard of them. Why did Carter ask you about them?"

"My name was on a list along with their names."

Jack tried but only managed to bite back half of the curses that flew to his mouth. "Where did Carter get the list?"

"He found it in Hal Hayden's hotel room. Carter told me the men were local criminals. It's obvious that Hal hired one of them to kill Nick and me."

"What's his motive?"

"Maybe Nick was breaking up with him."

"Did you see signs of that?"

"No, but I wasn't paying attention to the two of them. Mitchell would probably know."

"If they were breaking up, Hal might have killed Nick, but why you?" Jack asked. "And it was your name, not Nick's on the list."

"True, but jealousy and greed are the two most common motives for murder," Kelly said. "That was in my script once. Maybe Hal killed for greed. I know he liked the lifestyle Nick offered and he wasn't talented enough to ever reach that level of stardom on his own."

"And with Nick dead, he lost all of that. He definitely has no legal claim on Nick's estate."

"So what do I do, just sit around and wait for one of the guys on the list or some other piece of scum to try to kill me again? The next guy with a gun could be anywhere. In that car, in that one, in that one." Kelly pointed at every vehicle in sight.

On a scale of one to ten, her frustration level was probably kicking around at twenty and his wasn't far behind. The list had been found in Hal's hotel room, so it made sense that either Hal was behind it, or someone had set him up. But why?

Kelly turned and put a hand on his arm, all of a sudden excited again. "That must have been the list Nick was talking about in the hospital. He found out Hal was going to have me killed and when he confronted him with it, Hal shot him. That's it. Case solved."

"And Hal's motive for having you killed?"

"Do you have to be so hung up on that?"

"I just think there has to be more to this than we've ferreted out so far."

"Maybe it's not as complicated as the cases you usually investigate. My theory is the perfect explanation. And the best part of it is that if Hal were paying someone to kill me and now he's dead, the hit man won't bother to finish the job. I mean, what would be the point of committing the crime since the hit man either already has the money or won't be getting it?"

"That's a very neat package you've wrapped up."

"It makes sense, Jack."

Except that there was still no motive. He'd love to stop in town and smoke out one of his informants, but he couldn't risk taking Kelly into those areas. And as nicely wrapped as Kelly's package was, he wasn't at all sure it didn't have an explosive hidden under the shiny paper.

He checked the traffic behind him before steering the car into a U-turn. He couldn't take Kelly to smoke out the informants, so he'd have to settle for the next best thing.

Chapter Ten

Kelly had stopped being amazed at anything Jack and PPS were capable of, but it had been fascinating watching from a few doors down as Jack flashed his credentials and persuaded the young Asian woman cleaning room 1018 to open the door to room 1014.

"The yellow police tape you just ripped from the wall said Do Not Enter By Order Of Police," she said, once the cleaning woman had walked away.

"That's why I took it down. I'd never break the law."

"What did you say to the woman to get her to leave her cleaning cart and come open the door for you?"

"That I'm here to search the room of the recently deceased guest. I could have spouted the Pledge of Allegiance and gotten the same response. I don't think she understood a word of English. It was my PPS ID and my .38 that convinced her I was official."

"Or that you're a thief. She may be calling security right now."

"She's vacuuming. Just relax and keep thinking those positive thoughts you were having in the car."

But it was hard to stay positive as she stepped into the room and got a glimpse of the balcony where Hal had plunged to his death. Standing in this room and looking out, she could almost feel death.

Hal's death, Nick's death.

She swallowed hard and glanced around the room. It was in shambles. The drawers of the heavy wooden chest hung askew and the contents looked as if they'd been dumped and then stuffed in again with no attempt at order. A pair of boxer shorts dangled from one, a woolen muffler from another.

Kelly stepped over the pile of dirty sheets that had been left on the floor. "How can they say there's no sign of foul play when the room's trashed like this?"

"This is the work of Carter's boys. That's how they found the list with your name on it."

Hers and a couple of probable hit men. "What are we looking for?"

"I don't know," Jack admitted, "but I'll recognize it when I see it. We need to move quickly. I figured we'd have to fight our way through reporters, but I guess they just took their pictures and left. But anyone could show up at any time."

"From the looks of this room, I can't believe there could be a shred of evidence left."

"Sometimes the best investigators overlook something. And since no foul play was indicated, the room wouldn't have been combed by a CSI unit, which means there is even more chance of our finding a stray clue."

Kelly opened the closet door. It was taller than most hotel closets, built under a spot where the ceiling peaked. Hal's clothes were still hanging there, including the tuxedo he'd worn to the premiere Friday night. She sank her hands into the trouser pockets and felt around for whatever she might find. She came up with a piece of lint.

She kept going through his clothes, checking pockets. There were receipts, event tickets, scribbled notes that had no bearing on the case. But Hal was guilty. She knew it.

But what if she was wrong and the man with the assault rifle was waiting and watching for a second chance?

The heater kicked on, and a blast of hot air slapped her in the face, triggering a dull ache at her temples. "It's stuffy in here."

"Why don't you open the door to the balcony and let in a little fresh air," Nick called from the bathroom. She couldn't see him but she could hear him moving things around. She crossed the room again, unlocked the sliding-glass door and stepped outside.

The icy wind whipped around the corner of the building, howling so loudly that it all but drowned out the noise from the street ten stories below. It cut right though her jeans and sweater, and the ache at her temple intensified into a pulsing pain. She ducked back into the room for her coat. That helped, but her nose and cheeks were still freezing.

It must have been just as cold and windy last night when Hal stepped onto the balcony. But instead of retreating back into the warmth, he'd walked the few feet to the iron railing.

Kelly did the same, leaning over just enough to see the sidewalk below the balcony. It was stained with blood. She grew nauseous at the thought of his body being flattened against the hard pavement.

She stared shivering, and she couldn't stop. One minute alive. One minute dead. It had happened to Nick. It had happened to Hal. It could happen to anyone.

She looked over the edge again. A woman and little girl were walking hand-in-hand below her. They were laughing together as if they didn't have a care. Didn't they know that in an instant their lives could be torn apart and a killer could be firing at them on a lonely road?

"How much fresh air do you need? It's freezing out here."

She hadn't heard Jack approach, but she was keenly aware now of his nearness and his protective arm around her shoulders. "Do you watch over all your clients this well?"

"I don't remember pulling any of the others off a freezing balcony."

"I meant the way you're always here with a shoulder to lean on."

"No, the shoulder's just for you."

His voice grew husky. Must be the wind. She turned to press her face into the warmth of his sweater, but instead met his smoky gaze. The frigid wind still howled, but suddenly she was flushed with heat. Her fragile hold on her emotions slipped, and she reached up and wound her arms around Jack's neck.

She pressed against him, not thinking and not caring about what she was doing. She was so tired of fighting everything.

And then his lips were on hers, hungry, demanding, almost savage—the kind of kiss she hadn't known in a long, long time. She kissed him back, over and over, withholding nothing. She lost her breath to his, and still she didn't pull away.

But then, hot, ridiculous tears burned at the back of her eyelids and started running down her cheeks. She tried to bite them back, but they wouldn't stop. She pulled away from Jack and turned again to the balcony, holding on to the railing as sobs racked her body.

Finally the tears subsided, and she reached into her pocket for a tissue. Jack took it from her shaking fingers and wiped away her tears.

"I'm sorry," he said. "I was out of line, way out of line."

"Don't apologize. I kissed you. I don't know why. And I don't know why I cried. It just happened."

"You had a meltdown coming to you. You deserved it."

They left it like that and she returned to the closet, but this time pulled up a chair to use as step stool so that she could reach the very top shelf. She pulled down a quilt and an extra pillow and let them fall to the floor.

There was still something back there. She balanced on the arm of the chair, teetering as she stretched until she could get her fingers around whatever they'd brushed against.

Finally she had it in her grasp, but she let go and yanked her hand away. "Come here a minute, Jack. I found something."

He rushed from the chest where he'd been ravaging drawers. "What is it?"

"A gun. It's some kind of gun. You get it. I hate the feel of them."

Jack fumbled until he found it, then held it in front of him while he examined it. "A Browning nine millimeter. Good job, Kelly."

"I don't think anyone had looked behind the quilt and sheets. They gave up too soon."

"Actually, I'm ready to get out of here, too," Jack said.

"Good." She turned to grab her coat and noticed a square of paper on the floor by the chair that hadn't been there before. Evidently she'd knocked it from the shelf when she'd pulled down the bed linens. She picked it up and turned it over.

"What's that?" Jack asked, stepping closer so he could see what she was studying so intently.

"A photograph of me." She handed it to him. "It was taken recently, but I don't know when. I've only had that blouse a couple of months. Why would Hal Hayden carry around my picture?"

There was only one answer to that question, and she didn't need Jack to supply it. "My theory's right. I know it is. Hal showed this picture to the hit man so he'd know who to take out."

Jack was still standing there, holding the gun in one hand and her photo in the other when she heard a click behind her. She spun around just as the door swung open and a smirking Detective Gilly Carter stepped inside.

Sunday, 2:47 p.m.
PPS Headquarters

KELLY WAVED GOODBYE to Alex, but her daughter's attention had returned to the video she was watching on a small-screen TV. Alex looked quite contented, nestled in pillows that had been piled onto a love seat. Sara was perusing some files at the desk now, but it was clear in the ten minutes Kelly had spent visiting with them that Sara and Alex had bonded.

The hallway was empty as Kelly hurried to meet Jack. Gilly Carter had been furious at finding them in Hal Hayden's hotel room. He'd threatened to arrest both of them, but as Jack had explained on the way back to PPS, that would have meant his having to admit publicly that Jack had found evidence the DPD had overlooked.

Instead Carter had settled for confiscating the gun. She was sure he would have taken the picture of her, too, had he seen it. But if the gun had turned out to be the weapon used to kill Nick, both Jack and the detective would have to agree with her theory. Somehow Hal Hayden was behind all of this.

Kelly's mind slid back to the kiss she'd shared with him on the balcony. He'd brushed it all away as meltdown, but it had been more than that.

It was the way he'd been there for her every second since he'd walked back into her life. Fourteen years ago, he'd been the rebel, but he'd taken all that wild, restless energy and harnessed it into something strong and brave and good. He was a hero, a man among men. A man you could always count on. That's what Evangeline had been trying to tell her today.

She found Jack in the lounge already biting into a slice of piping hot pizza.

"How did you manage this? Even PPS can't get delivery that fast."

"The guys who were working today ordered in. This was an extra."

"I was thinking I'd be lucky to get stale crackers and peanut butter." She took her first bite and trailed a string of cheese from the paper plate to her mouth.

"Mmm." She licked a bit of the sauce from her

lips. "Messy but delicious." She finished that slice in record time and started on her second, stopping to wipe her mouth every few bites and still getting some sauce on her shirt.

"Good that your agent friends aren't in here to see how messy your client is."

Jack reached over and dabbed at her mouth with a clean napkin. "They could still be watching. You're on camera."

"You have cameras in the lounge?"

"We have cameras everywhere, so don't do anything inside these walls you don't want to show up on someone's monitor."

She scanned the room. "You're lying. I don't see any cameras in here."

"You see that can of mushroom soup on the shelf?"

"I see it, but you're not going to tell me that's a camera?"

"Takes a picture through a hole the size of a pin prick and shows a view of half the room."

"I'm impressed. Are there more?"

"A couple."

She wiped her mouth again, just in case. "Let me see if I can locate one." She scanned the room again, slowly this time. "Is that box of crackers a camera?"

"No."

"Is there one in the ceiling fan?"

"Not in this room."

She glanced at her watch. Mitchell should be arriving any minute. "Okay, I give up. Show me."

"The picture on the wall behind me of the two kids on skis."

"No way. That's a photograph."

"And a camera. It's in one of the snaps in the boy's jacket. And the fake electrical switch box by the door."

"It looks just like the real ones."

"That's the point."

She devoured her third slice of pizza before the pangs of hunger ceased. Jack was on his fourth and still going strong.

"Don't you think we can cancel the meeting with Mitchell since we know Hal killed Nick?"

"I know you want to believe this is over. Believe me, I do, too, but…"

"You have your doubts."

"There are too many unanswered questions."

And in spite of the list, the gun and the picture, he wasn't convinced. She could see it in his eyes and hear it in his voice. And just that fast the doubts crept back inside her.

"Okay, Jack, but I need to freshen up a bit before we meet with Mitchell. Is there a ladies' room nearby?"

"On the way to the conference room. Wait and I'll go with you. I'll have to unlock the door."

"Don't tell me there's an eye scan on the bathroom door?" she asked as she dropped her paper plate and napkins into the trash.

"No, just card access."

She thought he might be kidding, but when they

reached the restroom a few minutes later, he shoved a hotel-style key into the slot and two green lights flickered. She pushed through the door, then stopped.

"Everywhere *except* the bathroom," he assured her, then winked and left her to take care of business in the one room in PPS headquarters that fortunately had no hidden cameras.

JACK AND KELLY WERE SEATED in comfortable, upholstered chairs on opposite ends of the small oak conference table when Elisha ushered Mitchell into the sunlit room. The wear and tear of the last few days showed in his face and reminded Kelly how close he and Nick had been.

She stood and embraced him. "It's good to see you."

"You, too."

He exchanged greetings with Jack and took a seat, placing a black leather briefcase on the table before turning back to Kelly. "Have you decided to let me charter you a flight home tomorrow?"

The guy was very persistent, but then she already knew that about him. "Not at this point."

"I guess Kelly staying here is your recommendation, Mr. Sanders."

"It is, but I'm glad to hear you're concerned about Kelly and Alex. I know you'd like to see Nick's killer arrested almost as much as Kelly would."

Mitchell nodded. "I think that matter's best left to the Denver Police Department, but I'll answer your questions if I can."

"I appreciate that. Let's start with Hal Hayden. What do you know about his and Nick's relationship?"

"Nick gave him bit parts in his last two films, and they were friends."

So much for honesty, Kelly thought. And if Mitchell lied about that, how could they believe anything else he said? But then she really couldn't fault him for staying loyal to Nick.

"Were there problems in their relationship?" Jack continued.

"Aren't there in every relationship? Though I think friendship is the more appropriate terminology here."

"Let me rephrase that," Jack said. "Have any recent problems developed in their friendship?"

Mitchell crossed his arms in front of him. "I suppose I can tell you the same thing I told Detective Carter when he called this morning. Nick had some concerns that Hal was taking advantage of him."

"What made him think that?"

"Nick's very generous with all his friends. Cars, trips, season tickets to the Lakers. He bought me a new Porsche when I successfully negotiated his last contract. When times are good, he shares the wealth. That's just the way he is. I'm sure Kelly's told you that."

And when times were bad, he invested in get-rich-quick schemes—and still threw money around as if he printed it in the back room. But that was Nick.

"Since Nick and Hal were friends, he must have been generous with Hal, too," Jack said.

"Only Hal didn't wait for Nick to offer. He pushed

for things, and even bought things on his own and then expected Nick to pay for them."

"And they'd argued about this?"

"I don't know. Look, I really don't feel right talking about this with you. Whatever Nick did, he meant well, and I know too little about Hal to voice an opinion." He tuned his gaze to Kelly. "Don't you grieve for your husband at all, Kelly? Have you just written him off as if he never existed, as if he isn't Alex's father?"

"I'll grieve for him, Mitchell, in my own time, in my own way. I'll grieve for him when the fear shuts down and I don't have to think that he dragged my daughter into danger. I'll grieve for him then. Right now, I'm too busy making sure the two of us stay alive."

Tears burned at the back of her eyes, but she wouldn't give in to them this time. She didn't owe Mitchell an explanation of what she was going through right now.

"I'm sorry, Kelly. I didn't mean that the way you took it."

The tension in the room multiplied a hundredfold. If there had been a chance Mitchell would cooperate, it was probably lost now.

Jack stayed calm. She didn't know how he did it.

"I'm just going to lay it out straight, Mitchell. I'm clutching at straws, trying to protect Kelly and Alex. At this point I have to assume that Nick's murder and the attack on Kelly are related, so I have to look at Nick's life. And I have to ask questions. All I'm asking from you are some answers. They're not to desecrate Nick's memory. They're to save lives. So, please, level with me."

Mitchell nodded. "Okay."

"Are you aware that Nick was in serious financial trouble?"

"I know how much money he makes and that he must spend every penny of that supporting his lifestyle, but I'm not aware of how much he has in the bank or how much he owes. I expect the ratio is not good. He wasn't one of the top-paid actors. He just liked to live as if he were."

Surprisingly, it seemed as if Mitchell had decided to cooperate. Either her outburst or Jack's steady determination had gotten through to him.

"Do you know anything about his investments with TCM?" Jack asked.

Mitchell exhaled slowly as if he were releasing pure steam. "I warned him not to get involved with them the same way I've warned him about all those other investment schemes he falls into. Obviously, he didn't listen to me."

"Don't get upset by this next question, Mitchell. Just think it through, and try to be as honest as you can. It's important. Do you know of any business dealings Nick's been involved in that could possibly involve theft, blackmail, or any other criminal activity?"

"No, of course not. I would have stepped in if I'd thought he was into anything illegal. My reputation was tied up with his. If he goes down, I go down. That's the way it works in this business."

"Do you know of any bank accounts Nick opened outside the United States?"

"He's never mentioned any."

"Do you think it's even remotely possible that Hal Hayden killed Nick?"

"Hal? Why would he kill the goose that laid the golden egg?"

"Unless Kelly has something to add, I guess that covers it," Jack said.

"I have one question."

"Go ahead," Mitchell said.

"How long had Nick been taking amphetamines?"

"Ever since he started hanging out with Hal."

Kelly's chest tightened. "You were always so determined that Nick not do anything to blow his public image. If you knew he was taking drugs, why didn't you stop him?"

"I tried. He kept insisting he had everything under control, but he didn't, and he wasn't going to as long as Hal was around."

"Why didn't you mention the drugs to me?"

"Why would I? The only communication between the two of you concerned Alex, and this didn't affect her."

"I should have been the judge of that."

Mitchell stood and walked over to stand beside Kelly. "We both know Nick wasn't perfect, but he was a good man at heart. He loved life and had a hell of a lot of potential if he could have gotten his priorities straight. I'll miss him. I'll miss him a lot.

And, Kelly, I'm still here for you. If you need anything at all, just call."

"Thanks, Mitchell. I will call, and we'll get together soon."

She wondered if Nick had realized what a great
friend and champion he'd had in Mitchell Caruthers.

Sunday, 9:30 p.m.
The Single S

JACK STRETCHED and stared at his empty coffee cup
wondering if he dared add more caffeine to his
system. He'd been at the kitchen table for the last
three hours trying to make sense of all of this. The
evidence and clues were piling up, all pointing at Hal
Hayden, but missing several key pieces to the puzzle.

If Nick and Hal had argued after the premiere and
Nick had broken up with him, then Hal might well
have shot him in a crime of passion. But that didn't
explain a hit man for Kelly.

He heard Kelly stirring about the den. He'd
avoided her ever since they'd returned to the ranch,
even making an excuse not to have the supper of
soup and sandwiches with her and Alex.

He couldn't look at her now without thinking of
the kiss. It had become a tangible thing that hovered
between them whenever they were alone together.

The kiss brought it all back home for him. The
ride up Canyon Road was as vivid in his mind tonight

as it had been fourteen years ago. All that time, and she'd never once been out of his heart.

But that wasn't what today's kiss was about for Kelly.

He'd seen similar outbursts too often when he was in the army. One of your buddies gets killed and you go out and get laid. Not driven by love but by fear and walking too close to death. By the need for release.

She was vulnerable now, afraid and grieving for a man she hadn't loved, but who had nonetheless been part of her life. She needed a friend—might even need more, like strong arms to hold her while she cried. What she didn't need was all his pent-up emotion dumped on her. Her needs were temporary. His had been nurtured by memories and longing for fourteen years.

He heard Kelly's footfalls behind him, but didn't look up, not even when he felt her hand on his shoulder.

"Jack." Her fingers trailed the back of his neck, and in spite of his good intentions he had to fight to keep from turning and pulling her into his arms.

"Yeah."

"Do you remember that night on Canyon Road?"

Chapter Eleven

Jack's breath burned in his lungs as he fought the overwhelming attraction. If he looked at Kelly, he'd kiss her. If he kissed her, it would never stop there.

"You were the forbidden man about campus, the guy who didn't follow anyone's rules. The guy who took risks and lived on the edge. The guy mothers warned you about and fathers forbade you to go near. Going with you that night was the most daring and thrilling thing I'd ever done."

"I was just a kid who was too dumb to steer clear of trouble."

"Not in my mind. When I climbed on your bike that night, I wanted to ride forever, just you and me, fast and flying around the curves. But then you rode your bike off the road and stopped on the very edge of the canyon. We climbed off and you put your windbreaker on the grass for me to sit on. Do you remember what you said then?"

"No." All he remembered was the blood rushing to his head and thinking he'd go crazy if he didn't have her—the same as he felt right now.

"You told me to look at the sky. There were a million stars, twinkling like diamonds. And you said that I sparkled more brilliantly than any of them."

"I said that?"

"Word for word."

"How do you remember all of that?"

"I locked all the memories from that night away in my mind. I was afraid I might never feel that kind of magic again."

Jack was losing ground fast. Still he had to push to stay sane. "You think things like that at eighteen."

Her thumbs trailed his earlobes. "I'm thirty-two years old, Jack Sanders. I'm still waiting to feel that kind of passion again."

"Kelly." Her name was a moan on his lips. In every dream, through countless army rescue missions, through nights shattered by death and enemy fire, it had always been thoughts of Kelly that had got him through. The memories merged with reality as he gave up the battle to resist.

He stood and pulled her into his arms. A warning went off in his head. But the warning was too little, and much too late. He claimed her mouth, kissing her over and over, aching with a need more intense than any he'd ever known.

Her fingers twisted in his hair and her arms wound tightly around his neck. She was pressed against him, so close he could feel her heart beating. He roamed her back with his hands, then slid them beneath her sweater and splayed his fingers against her soft skin.

He fought the impulse to take her right here on the kitchen floor, to take her wildly the way they'd made love on Canyon Road.

Her hand slipped between his thighs, and his heart beat so loudly it almost overrode the sudden piercing ring of his phone.

"Let it ring," Kelly whispered. "Just let it ring."

He tried, but his sense of responsibility finally got through his passion-fogged brain. "I have to see who it is, but don't go away. I'll be right back."

He checked the ID. Damn. There was no way he could let the call go unanswered.

"Jack, it's Karen Butte. I'm glad I caught you."

"What's up?"

"Did I interrupt anything important? You sound winded."

"I can talk."

"I have to make this quick. Are you involved with Nick Warner's murder in any way?"

"I'm protecting his wife and daughter."

"I surmised as much since you were in their hotel suite Friday morning."

"Why the call?"

"I need some information from Nick's wife about

his investments. I wouldn't ask her at a time like this, if it wasn't a matter of life and death."

"Whose life?"

"I can't talk now." Her voice dropped to a whisper. "Tomorrow morning. Meet me at 227 Spruce Drive, apartment 204-B, nine o'clock."

She broke the connection before he could ask more. Karen Butte was used to playing hardball, but she was nervous tonight. Or scared. Something big was about to blow, and whatever it was involved Nick Warner and possibly Kelly.

"Who were you talking to? You look upset."

Upset and consumed again with keeping her from the hands of a killer. The moment between the two of them had passed. But they'd crossed a line that allowed no going back. And no way to go forward until the danger was over and he was certain Kelly and Alex were safe.

Then, whether they made love or not, Kelly would go back to her life in Beverly Hills, and he'd be left to spend another fourteen years trying to forget her.

Monday, 8:47 a.m.
En route to Karen Butte's apartment

KELLY WAS APPREHENSIVE yet hopeful, running on adrenaline and caffeine that overrode her fatigue. She'd lain awake for hours last night, one minute haunted by the horrors of the last three days, the next drowning in erotic thoughts of Jack.

It might be wrong to have such sensual urges when her life was in total chaos and the man she'd called her husband wasn't even in the ground. But life had never seemed more fragile and precious, and she wouldn't let herself be sorry for being alive and feeling passion in her soul.

Whatever happened between her and Jack, she refused to let it be sullied by regrets or misplaced guilt.

Jack had wanted her to stay at the ranch with Alex and the PPS agent who had reported for duty. She'd insisted she go with him, and finally he'd given in. After all, she was the one the investigative reporter wanted to talk to. Her being there might help bring this all to an end.

"I think this meeting with Karen Butte is going to be the turning point," she said, breaking the silence that had ridden with them since they'd driven out the back gate of the Single S.

"I hope you're right, but there's no guarantee her investigation has anything to do with Nick's death. More likely it's an exposé on fly-by-night companies who suck in naive investors."

"If you believed that you wouldn't have called Cameron Morgan to come stay with Alex. You'd have blown Karen off until this was over or had her meet you at PPS at your convenience."

"You're picking up on all my tricks."

"I really do think this is going to come to a head today. What Karen's going to tell us combined with what you and Lenny have discovered will fit together and give you the pieces to solve the puzzle."

"Karen said she wanted to *ask* questions. She may not tell us anything."

"Are you always so negative?"

"I just hate for you to count too much on this being the end-all when it might be a dead end."

"Lenny said you are the master at taking isolated facts and fitting them into the complete whole."

"Lenny exaggerates."

"And you're modest."

"Does this mean you've given up on Hal being the killer?" Jack asked.

"Nope. I think Karen is going to supply us with that elusive motive you keep talking about."

"You are optimistic today."

"I am about this. I'm a little more concerned about Cameron handling Alex until we get back to the ranch. She was already wrapping him around her little finger when we left. She probably talked him into ice cream and cookies for breakfast."

"He'd never do that. Beer maybe, ice cream, never."

"That does not make me feel better." Jack was trying to keep things light, but he'd been so upset after Karen's call last night that his lustful passion had been transformed into an all-business protective surge. He'd been tense ever since, and she knew he didn't share her optimism.

Kelly's phone rang. She expected it to be Mitchell calling to badger her about returning to Los Angeles.

Worse. It was her mom. She was tempted not to answer, but that would send her parents into a panic attack, and she couldn't do that to them.

"Hi, Mom."

"I just saw the news. They said that actor who fell from his hotel balcony was a friend of Nick's."

"They were friends, but Hal's fall was just one of those freak accidents that happen sometimes."

"The reporter said he might not have fallen, that he could have been pushed."

News to Kelly. "He was just speculating, Mom. You know how they try to make everything a big news story."

"I'm worried, Kelly, really worried." Her voice broke.

"Don't do this, Mom. Please don't cry. I'm fine and so is Alex. I'd tell you if we weren't."

"Are you still staying at that bodyguard's ranch?"

"Yes, and you wouldn't believe the high-tech equipment he has there. He knows if a leaf blows a hundred yards away."

"Don't humor me, Kelly. We're coming out there. Your father is on the computer right now getting—"

The phone cut out. "Darn!"

"What's wrong?"

"My phone's dead. With all that's going on, I forgot to recharge the battery."

"Here." He handed her his phone. "But make it quick. We're only a few blocks from Karen's apartment."

There was no making it quick. She had to get her father on the phone and persuade him not to click the submit button on his ticket purchase. She succeeded as they were hurrying up the stairs to apartment 204-B.

Kelly had her first intimation that this might not go as she'd hoped when there was no answer at the door.

"Maybe the doorbell's broken," she said.

Jack pounded on the door, but still there was no response. He tried the knob. It turned, so he pushed the door open and she followed him inside.

And there was Karen Butte lying in the middle of the floor, a bullet through her head.

JACK STEPPED OVER a stream of blood and walked to where he had a better view of the body. Karen had been shot twice when either bullet would have spilled her brains onto the carpet. This had *hit* written all over it.

"Don't touch anything," he warned.

"I wouldn't."

Kelly was standing behind him. When he turned, he saw that her face was pasty-white.

"Call 911," she urged.

"It's too late for that."

"Then call the cops."

"I'll call them as we leave." Kelly was hanging in there but he didn't want to leave her standing alone and staring at the body while he searched the apartment.

"Ready for another Easter egg hunt?"

"If it helps."

Jack went to the kitchen, located some plastic freezer bags and handed two to Kelly. "Put these on your hands like mittens, but still be careful what you touch. We don't want to smudge finger-prints, though I doubt there are any. You can start in the bedroom."

"What do I look for?"

"Anything with Nick's name on it. I'll take Karen's office. She's freelance, so I'm sure she has one."

Her office had been ransacked as he'd expected. There was a computer monitor on Karen's desk, but no computer. There was an adapter for a laptop, but no laptop. Files were scattered about the floor. The room had been combed by someone who probably knew exactly what he was looking for.

Jack searched anyway, getting angrier by the second. This was his town. He should know what was going on. He should know who called for a hit and why. He should know who'd ambushed them on the way to the airport.

He should know—but he didn't.

The equipment at PPS was state-of-the-art, but this case wasn't going to be solved at headquarters. Jack was taking it to the streets, and Kelly would not be going with him. He found her in the bedroom staring at a photograph of Karen receiving some kind of award. "Let's get out of here," he said.

He put his arm around Kelly's shoulders, wishing she hadn't seen this, hating Nick for dragging her into whatever sordid mess he'd become involved with. "I'll call the cops. They'll contact her next of kin."

His phone vibrated as he led Kelly to the door. He waited until they reached the car before checking it. A text message from Karen Butte.

Milo Kardascian.

Kelly looked over his shoulder. "Who is Milo Kardascian?"

"I have no idea, but the message is from Karen."

"When did she leave it?"

"At 8:52 a.m."

"Oh, God, Jack, she died while I was using your phone. We were only blocks from her apartment. If we'd left the ranch a few minutes sooner, if we hadn't hit so many red lights, if…" She shuddered. "We must have barely missed the killer."

"Looks that way."

"She couldn't' have keyed in the message while she was dying—not with the top of her head blown away."

"No, she died instantly," he assured.

"So she knew she was about to die, and still she had the presence of mind to type someone's name. It has to be a clue to what she was investigating—a very important clue."

"Definitely worth checking into."

"What will you do now?"

"Find out who Milo Kardascian is." And go looking for a killer.

Monday, 11:06 a.m.
PPS Headquarters.

KELLY HAD BEEN DISTRAUGHT when they'd left Karen Butte's apartment. Jack had been insistent that he couldn't protect her on the Denver streets while he smoked out an informant. Still, she'd begged to go with him—until he'd reminded her that if she got killed, Alex would be an orphan. That had instantly put things back into perspective.

With the blizzard forecast to move in by morning, she'd suggested he drop her off at PPS headquarters rather than waste precious time driving all the way back to the ranch before hitting the streets. But she hadn't sat around doing nothing. And what she'd found had her more convinced than ever of Hal's guilt.

"You know, Kelly, you may have actually cracked this case," Lenny said, as he dropped the faxed copy of Nick's recently revised will on Jack's desk. "All on your own, too. Checking Nick's will wasn't at the top of my to-do list."

"Nor mine, until I decided to call Olivia Turner. Of course it took twenty minutes of listening to her rave about her fabulous postpremiere soirée Friday night at her estate before I could get her to hear anything I was saying."

"I'm still not sure I have all that straight. How did Olivia overhear Nick and Hal arguing when our agent at that same party had only seen them laughing together?" Lenny frowned.

"Olivia had invited Drake Patton upstairs to show him the frieze a local craftsman had carved in the ceiling of her boudoir. They walked in on Hal and Nick in a heated argument. That's all I got from her."

"Then it was Drake who actually alerted you to the will?"

"Exactly. He said Nick was slurring his words, that he was drunk or high on something."

"The speed they found in his blood."

"Right, pills that he'd probably gotten from Hal. Anyway, as Nick was bolting from the room, he spewed that the will would be changed by morning."

"It seems that Drake would have called the police or at least called you when he heard about Nick being murdered."

"His own movie was being premiered the next evening. I'm sure that claimed all his attention. Besides, like he said, he would never have suspected Hal of murder. He'd assumed Nick's death was from a robbery gone bad."

Kelly picked up Nick's recently revised will to read it for herself, though the attorney had already given her the meat of it over the phone.

One-third of Nick's estate—such as it was—was to go into a trust fund for Alex. One-third was to go to Mitchell Caruthers for his years of dedicated service. And one-third would go to Kelly, up until the date that she died or filed for divorce. After said filing or death, the one-third designated for her would go to Hal Hayden.

Nick would never have expected to die before she divorced him, but that provision must have satisfied some sense of legal obligation. Unfortunately, that phrase had almost cost three lives. With Nick dead, Hal realized there would be no divorce, so his only way to collect what he must have thought was a fortune was for Kelly to die, too.

The *motive*.

"I keep thinking about timing," Lenny said. "It would be close, but it could work if Hal got Degrazia's and Sheffield's names right after he killed Nick. That would still leave him a few hours to line up one of them and give them time to be waiting for you and Jack when you were driving to the airport, provided he knew your travel plans."

"I'm sure he got that information from Mitchell," she said, "but where would he have gotten Degrazia's and Sheffield's names?"

"That's easy enough," Lenny said. "All you have to do is hit a honky-tonk on the other side of the tracks, down in the area where Jack is right now."

Lenny picked up the mug of lukewarm coffee he'd been carrying around the last half hour, then set it back down without taking a drink. "I'm just not sure how Karen Butte fits into this."

"My take at this point is that she was investigating one or more of the sleazy companies Nick had invested in, and she needed to know about his involvement. That might or might not be the story that got her killed."

Lenny nodded. "That theory has some merit. What about the man who broke into the rented house in the wee hours of Friday morning? That wouldn't have been Hal."

Damn, how could she have forgotten that? But she refused to let one little loose end rain on her parade. Hal was the killer. She'd discovered his motive.

Jack would have to be impressed.

Monday, 11:52 a.m.
Denver Streets

THE BAR WAS GRIMY, the floor marred from boots and cigarette burns. And even in the dim light that filtered through the filthy window, Jack could see the layers of muck on the bar stools and smell the puke of one of last night's drunks.

Jack had spent the last two hours going from one to another of his favorite informant's regular hangouts and this was the most disgusting so far.

"You looking for somebody?"

Jack could barely hear the question over the loud rap music coming from the cheap overhead speakers. "I'm looking for Snarky."

"I don't know no Snarky."

"Snarky Jefferson."

"Still don't know him."

"I got a twenty-dollar bill says you do."

The guy was perched on the edge of a bar stool, leaning over a porn magazine that looked as if it had been in and out of a lot of filthy hands. He needed a shave and a shower and a shirt that had been washed this year. Jack was in this area fairly often, but he was pretty sure he'd never seen this particular degenerate before.

"If I was to know this Snarky, who would I say is looking for him?"

"An old friend."

"You a cop?"

"Nope."

"You look like a cop. Talk like one, too. You totin'?"

"You got people walk through this neighborhood without a weapon?"

"Not for long. What kind of business you got with Snarky?"

The jerk knew where Snarky was. He was messing with Jack now, and Jack was fast losing his patience. He knew the game, but he was tired of playing it. He yanked his gun from the shoulder holster under his jacket and pushed the barrel into the man's stomach. With his other hand, he grabbed the neck of the guy's shirt, twisting until he was gasping for air.

"I said I need to see Snarky."

The guy had to squeak out his response. "Try Laranelle's."

Jack tightened the twist. "Wouldn't be good if I found out you were lying to me."

The guy squeaked again, this time something incoherent. Jack let go of him, returned his weapon to its holster and walked out. Laranelle was legend. She had been the girlfriend of half the men who lived in this section of town where cocaine was king. Jack knew where she lived and where she worked. He'd killed a guy once in her bedroom. The guy had drawn first.

Jack walked the two blocks to her house, watching his back, though no one usually messed with him this time of the day. The ones who'd have cut his throat for money for their next fix were still asleep and recuperating from their last one.

Jack tapped on Laranelle's front door. He saw the curtain being pulled back at the front window before he heard the dead bolt click. Snarky opened the door a crack. "What you doing here, man? I'm trying to sleep."

"Looking for information."

"Walk around to the back. I don't want the bitch to wake up and find us talking."

Jack followed Snarky into a run-down garage behind the house.

"You got a smoke, man? This time of the morning, I need my smoke."

Jack didn't smoke but he carried a pack for situations like this. He shook the pack and stuck it out for Snarky to take one, then offered him a light. Snarky puffed and leaned against an old Chevy that was up on blocks.

"What kind of information you looking for?"

"Ever heard of a man named Milo Kardascian?"

"Naw. No Kardascian down here."

Snarky didn't always talk to Jack, but when he

did, he told the truth. Jack paid him well, and Snarky owed Jack for saving his son's life one night when the teenager had gotten into a knife fight near where Jack had been meeting another snitch. Snarky had been his chief informant ever since.

"So tell me about Billy Sheffield. Is he staying clean?"

"Far as I know. Causes hell on the streets and beats up his old lady, but he ain't in jail."

"Did he do a hit for somebody this past weekend?"

"You talking about that movie star guy wanting his wife taken out?"

"Could be. You got a name for the movie star?"

"Same one who they keep talking about on the TV, but looks like his old lady got to him first."

"Are you talking about Nick Warner?"

"That's the one. The big shot came down here a week ago and offered fifty thousand to have her bumped off. We got people here that would've done it for ten."

"Billy take the fifty?"

"Naw. He was ready to, till he heard the whole story."

"What was that?"

"Woman was going to have a kid with her most of the time. Billy, he's a ladies' man, you know."

"Like you?"

"Yeah, but not as good as I am where it counts. Know what I mean?"

Snarky laughed shakily. He was never easy when

he was squealing. He knew all too well what happened to snitches if they got caught by their peers.

"Billy didn't like the idea of killing off a woman to start with. But a kid? That's a hundred times worse. You know what they do to kid killers in prison? It ain't pretty."

"So what did Billy do?"

"Told the guy to find somebody else."

"Degrazia?"

"Maybe. Degrazia would shoot his own mother for fifty grand."

"Have you seen Degrazia around town?"

"Me, personally? No, man. But Laranelle said he came by the club where she dances a couple of nights ago."

"And Billy was sure that the man who wanted Mrs. Warner killed was her husband?"

"I just know what he told me."

"Where do I find Billy?"

Snarky coughed, a hoarse noise that sounded as if the lining was being stripped from his throat. He wiped his mouth on the sleeve of his shirt. "Don't let him know I told you anything."

"Of course not." Snarky gave him a couple of locations where he might find Billy.

"And where do I find Degrazia?"

"I don't know, but I wouldn't go looking if I were you. Mess with Degrazia, they don't ever find your body. And word on the street is he left town in a big hurry Saturday afternoon."

Jack paid Snarky cash and left to go find Billy Sheffield.

It took a while, but Jack finally found Billy smoking pot in a run-down park near where Snarky had told him Billy's mother lived. It took serious cash and some unfriendly persuasion to get him to talk. He finally agreed, but only because he hadn't committed the crime.

Jack took the photograph Kelly had found in Hal's closet from his shirt pocket. "Is this the woman Nick Warner wanted you to kill?"

"That's her. Same picture, in fact." Billy reached in his pocket and pulled out a duplicate of the photograph.

"What did the husband look like?"

"Just like he does on TV."

"And you talked to him personally?"

"Hell no. You think big-shot movie stars talk to people like me? They got flunkies for that. He talked to me on the phone to set up the deal, but when he come to bring the earnest money, he sat in a limousine with his tinted windows all rolled up."

"It's hard to identify a man behind tinted windows."

"He rolled the window down and hollered at his flunky when he wasn't quick enough getting back to the car. Guess big movie-star man was getting nervous down here on the streets."

"Did you take the money?"

"I checked to see if it was all there, but then when he mentioned the woman's kid might be with her, I threw it back at him. I figure a man might have reason to kill his wife, but what kind of monster would let his own kid go down with her?"

What kind of monster? The kind who had fathered Alex. This was going to tear Kelly apart. Jack pulled the payoff from his back pocket. "I appreciate the help, Billy."

"I ain't killing no woman with a kid. I got a few scruples."

Nick Warner had even fewer.

"One other thing," Billy said as Jack was walking away. "Another twenty-dollar bill and I'll give you the real kicker to this story."

"Better be worth it." Jack pulled another twenty from his pocket.

"The guy wanted me to break in on his wife one night before I killed her. He said shake her up a little, but don't hurt her, just act like I was looking for him. A decoy he said. What the hell was that about?"

A decoy so that Nick wouldn't be the first suspect they looked at. He'd thought of everything, only someone had got to him first.

Jack called Lenny on the way back to PPS to give him a heads-up. Lenny filled him in on what Kelly had learned.

Sonofabitch! She'd completely settled in on Hal as the one who'd tried to kill her. Now he had to tell her that it had been Nick who'd put a fifty-thousand-dollar price on her head.

"I need one more thing, Lenny."

"I know. Insurance. I'm already checking it out."

"And don't mention what I found out to Kelly."

"No, that ugly job is all yours."

Good thing Nick Warner was dead. If he hadn't been, Jack might have killed him with his bare hands.

Chapter Twelve

Monday, 1:30 p.m.
Road to Single S

Kelly was still talking excitedly as they turned on the narrow road that led to the back entrance of the ranch. Jack saw no reason to burst her bubble until he had to, which would be any minute now. He wouldn't want to give her that kind of news with Alex around.

This would hit her hard, though her resilience and determination over the last few days had been nothing short of spectacular.

"Gotta hand it to you," he said, when she finished telling of her morning's activities, "you're something else."

"Thank you, Agent Sanders. I was thrilled to finally be doing something useful instead of watching everyone else work while I wallowed in guilt, grief and fear."

"What could you possibly feel guilty about, surely not our kiss? You said you and Nick haven't been intimate in years, that you lived separate lives."

"No guilt for the kiss. But the guilt is about Nick. I keep thinking about what Mitchell said. You know, how I'm not showing the proper grief. I guess maybe I'm not, but I do feel terrible that Nick was murdered. Even if I had hated him—which I didn't—I'd never wish anything like that on Alex's father."

Here she was beating herself up for not grieving appropriately for a man who'd paid to have her killed. Now Jack was even more worried about what his news would do to her. All her efforts to spin Nick into a decent person and a good and loving father would go down the toilet.

"It's starting to snow again," she said. "Have you heard a recent weather forecast?"

"They've backed off a bit from the severe blizzard conditions, but they are expecting heavy snowfall tonight, and they're recommending that you be off the roads by dark unless you have urgent business."

"It's been a long time since I've been in a blizzard. What do you do when you're snowed in?"

"I'm usually snowed in at headquarters. I work."

"Why is that?"

"Have to have agents in the facility to take care of emergencies. I'm Single Sanders with no family, so I volunteer with the other lonely hearts."

"Single Sanders? Is that where the name of your ranch comes from?"

"Exactly. It has a nice ring, don't you think?"

"No. What if you get married, then what? Will you call it Married S?"

"I figure that's a bridge I can cross when and if I come to it."

Kelly leaned back and pulled one foot into the seat with her, the way she did when she was ready to get comfortable. He was learning all her little idiosyncrasies. The way she bit her bottom lip when she worried, the way she hugged her coffee mug instead of using the handle, the way she sucked on her spoon when she finished a bite of something cold.

So many memories to haunt him when she was gone. Newer, fresher memories of a grown-up Kelly to add to the ones from Lake Tahoe and Canyon Road.

"Why did you never try to get in touch with me after that night on Canyon Road?"

Her timing was uncanny, as if she'd been reading his mind again. He could never be as honest about his emotions as she was. She said what she thought and put her feelings right out there to be trampled on by men like Nick. Jack kept his tamped down, roped in, so that they didn't get trampled by anyone. Maybe that's why he was Single Sanders.

"I left for boot camp the next day," he said, coming up with an answer that was pure avoidance even though it was true. "While you were sunning in that little sky-blue bikini, I was doing push-ups and marching under a blazing sun."

"Did I have a sky-blue bikini?"

"Now who has the better memory?"

"You still could have written—or called?"

As if he hadn't thought about doing either or both a thousand times a day. "Why didn't you get in touch with me?"

"I think I was afraid."

"Smart thinking. I was a dangerous boy," he teased.

"You were, but that wasn't what frightened me. I was determined to become an actress, and I was afraid if I got too entangled with you, I'd end up married and pregnant."

"Actress-married-pregnant. Now you've done them all."

"And failed at two out of three. Not a great record."

"Ah, but you have your passions."

"Thank goodness."

"Is Drake Patton one of them?"

"Hardly, whatever gave you that idea?"

"The way he looked at you at the premiere Friday night."

"That's his sultry screen look. It means nothing. We're just friends, but he has voluntarily done some promotional videos for Chance for Children, and that is one of my passions. The other is Alex."

Jack was relieved to hear that Drake was just a friend, but it didn't change anything. He was too much a realist to think he and Kelly could ever make it together long term. It was as evident now as it had been back then. "You were out of my league in those days, Kelly. I knew that and so did your dad. He would have hanged me if he'd known what we did that night. You never told him, did you?"

"Are you crazy? I haven't even admitted to him that you're my bodyguard and I've been out from under his roof for fourteen years. But I'm not looking for his approval anymore," she said, "just in case you were worried about that."

He wasn't. His biggest worry right now was her reaction to what he'd learned about Nick. But it was better coming from him than someone else. His other worries weren't as pressing but the unanswered questions in this case bothered him nonetheless.

Karen Butte's murder and the fact that she'd seemed desperate to talk to Kelly about Nick. Nick's dying words about a list that might or might not be the list that linked Kelly to the hit men. The un-accounted-for two million dollars from the Puerto Escondido deal which might have triggered Nick's trying to tell Kelly something about TCM.

He might never find the answers to all of them, but he had a nagging suspicion they were going to come back into play.

They pulled up to the back gate and he released the lock with the control on his key ring. The same control told him that neither the front nor the back gate had been opened since they'd been gone.

"Home again," Kelly said. "I can't wait to see Alex, and then have a glass of wine by the fire without having to fear when and where the man with the assault rifle will show up next."

He couldn't put off the inevitable any longer. He stopped the car in the middle of the dirt road and killed the engine.

"We need to talk."

ONE LOOK INTO JACK'S dark, troubled eyes, and Kelly knew something was seriously wrong. Her apprehension swelled. "What is it?"

"I found out some new information today about our man with the assault rifle."

"What else can there be? Hal hired him to kill me. You saved our lives. Hal's dead. It's over and done with." She was talking too fast, letting the sentences spill over her lips like a waterfall. But it *was* over and done with and she didn't want him complicating things again.

"Hal probably killed Nick, just as you said, but he didn't hire the hit man. That was all arranged before you arrived in Denver."

"No. It was Hal. He had a motive. You said all my theory was missing was his motive, and I found it."

Jack stretched his arm across the back of the seat and laid his hand on her shoulder. "I know this will be hard to take, but I have to tell you the truth. It was Nick who hired the hit man, Kelly. He made a trip to Denver a week before the film festival and made a deal for your rented house to be broken into and for you to be killed."

"I was the one who insisted he rent the house. He wanted to stay in the hotel."

"When did you make that decision?"

"A few weeks ago…" Which didn't disprove anything. "The killer fired on us with Alex in the car. Even if Nick had wanted me dead, which is ludicrous, he would never have made an arrangement that could possibly harm Alex. He adored her."

But Jack believed differently. It was there in his eyes. She started to shake. "Who told you these things?"

"A man Nick approached to do the job."

"He could be a psycho like Bates. He might have been lying about being approached."

"He wasn't lying."

"How can you be so certain?"

"Because it's my job to know. And because the man he approached still had a duplicate of the photo you found in Hal's room."

"See? That proves it was Hal."

Jack massaged her shoulder with his fingertips, but even Jack's touch wasn't helping to calm the quaking now.

"It wasn't Hal who hired the hit man, Kelly, but I think he was in it with Nick. That's why he had the names of possible hit men and why he had your picture. It may have even been his idea, but it was Nick who offered the money."

"How much?"

"That's not—"

"I want to know how much, Jack. How much money was Nick willing to pay to have me killed?"

"Fifty thousand."

"He was in debt to his eyeballs. Why would he spend that kind of money to have me killed when I'd asked for a divorce six months ago? I wanted out of his way, out of his house, out of his life. He's the one who begged me to stay."

She threw up her hands. "Why? Why, Jack? You keep harping on motive. What was Nick's motive? I didn't have a legal claim to one penny of his money. All he'd have to give me was child support, and that would have been a lot cheaper than the clothes he wanted me to wear to his stupid Hollywood functions. So tell me why he wanted me dead."

"He took out a three-million-dollar life insurance policy on you five months ago."

"Wouldn't that make him a logical suspect in my death?"

"Which is why he concocted the story of the stalker and had someone break into the rented house. It would have transferred suspicion from him to a phantom stalker."

"No wonder he left me in his will. That made him look good, too. And as for this being Hal's idea, that only makes it worse. I'd been with Nick five years, helping to quell the rumors, giving birth to and raising his daughter, smiling at the ever-present paparazzi.

"Hal waltzes into Nick's life six months ago, tells him to have me killed, and Nick does—or at least he would have, if it hadn't been for you. I can't believe he hired you in the first place."

"More reason not to suspect him in your death."

"You said the hit man you talked to turned Nick down. Did he say why?"

Jack looked away, clearly not wanting to answer the question. But she'd heard the worst, she might as well hear the rest. "Tell me, Jack. What was it? Was I too risky? Did Nick have too many rules? Was that not enough money?"

Jack finally let their gazes meet. "Nick made it known that you were almost always with Alex, and that killing you might necessitate killing her, as well."

Kelly went ballistic. "How could he? He was her father. He loved her." Quick, hot tears squeezed from her eyes. "Oh, Jack, how could he pay someone to kill my precious Alex?"

Jack tried to pull her into his arms but she jumped from the car and started running down the road, running as hard and as fast as she could. She didn't want to be comforted. She didn't want to cry. All she wanted was to keep running until she passed out from exhaustion. Run until she couldn't think about Nick or murder or how much she hated him right now.

She didn't stop running until she'd burst through the door of Jack's house and swept Alex up in her arms. She swung her around, holding her tight, and not letting her go until she fell with her to the leather sofa.

"That was fun," Alex squealed. "Do it again."

"In a bit." Kelly snuggled Alex and kissed her on the cheek.

"Your nose is cold, Mommy."

"I know."

"Were you out making a snowman?"

"No, just jogging."

"Cameron and me made a snow dog, kind of like Stormy, but his tail kept falling off. And Cameron let me have three gooey marshmallows in my chocolate."

"Three. Wow!"

Alex heard Jack come in the back door and ran to tell him about the snow puppy and the three gooey marshmallows. Kelly huddled by the fire, out of breath and cold to the bone.

Jack came into the den where she stood shivering by the fire. "Your mother called on your cell phone while you were running back to the house. I answered and took a message. She wants you to call her."

"I don't want to talk to her right now."

"I think you may have to. She and your father are in Denver and they want to see you."

"I told them not to come."

"Do you think you'd stay away if you thought Alex was in danger, no matter how old she was?"

Kelly sighed, took the phone from his hand and made the call. "Hi, Mom."

"You don't sound like yourself. Have you been crying?"

"No. I think I may be coming down with a cold."

"Drink lots of orange juice."

"I thought we agreed that you and Dad wouldn't come to Denver."

"We're worried about you and Alex."

"You don't have to be worried anymore. Everything's taken care of. The danger's over and done with."

"Did they arrest the man who killed Nick?"

"I'll explain it all later."

"Then you don't need a bodyguard?"

"Right."

"Thank God! Your father has a rental car. We'll come get you and Alex and you and can spend the night here in the hotel, with us."

"Hold on a minute, Mom, I may be able to save you the trip out here." She caught Cameron just as he was leaving. "Are you going back into town?"

"Yeah, I've got some things to check on at headquarters."

"Could you stand having company for the drive?"

Monday, 2:15 p.m.
Single S Ranch

KELLY STOOD JUST OUTSIDE the door, watching Alex wave from the backseat of Cameron's car. She was excited about spending the night with her grandparents at the hotel, and they were thrilled she was coming. It had soothed their disappointment that Kelly had refused their invitation.

She wasn't up to talking to her parents, so Jack was stuck with her and her terrible mood for the night. The Single S had been her haven of safety. Now it had become her refuge from the storm, both literally and figuratively.

Nick and Hal had plotted to have her killed even if it meant killing Alex. It was horribly sick and twisted. But both Nick and Hal were dead and that news must have surely reached the paid killer by now. He'd be on the run, fifty thousand dollars richer even though Jack had foiled the attempt on her life. The danger to her and Alex was over.

The snowfall was still light, but the tempest inside Kelly was raging. She went searching for Jack and found him at his computer.

"Will you saddle the sorrel I rode Saturday? I'd like to take a ride before the weather worsens."

"Sure. Am I invited to go along?"

"You can go if you like. I'll be lousy company."

"We don't have to talk."

She went to change into warmer clothes without saying more. Her muscles were tight knots, it hurt to breathe and she felt as if she might throw up any minute. She's always heard that decent, everyday people could be driven to the kind of rage that made them take someone's life.

But Nick hadn't been in a state of rage when he'd decided she and Alex were disposable. He'd just calmly gone to Denver and offered someone money to have them erased from existence. And when the first hit man on his list had turned him down he'd simply gone to the next one.

Jack was waiting at the back door after she'd changed. He held her parka while she shoved her arms through the sleeves.

"You'll need this," he said, handing her a thick woolen muffler. "It's warmer than yours."

"Thanks."

"You should ride Ishwar," he said, when they reached the stables. "She loves a good gallop on a cold day and she's sure-footed and responds well to her rider."

He saddled a solid black horse for himself. He talked to both horses, calling them by name in the same soothing tone he'd been using on her.

In minutes they were riding across the rugged terrain. The cold wind stung her face and snowflakes stuck to her eyelashes. She pushed Ishwar to a gallop, thankful for the bitter cold and the punishing wind that pushed bracing air into her clogged lungs.

Hate. Kill. Hate. Kill. The words raced through her brain like a madman's mantra. Nick wanted them dead. They would have been dead. Dead if not for Jack. She screamed into the wind and let her frustration and fury echo all around them.

She could have ridden like that forever. Ishwar couldn't. When he slowed to a trot, they were high on a hilltop looking over a valley that stretched below them and the mountains in the distance.

"It's breathtaking," she said as Jack rode up behind her.

"This was the view that closed the sell on the ranch. Once I saw it, I knew this is where I was meant to be."

"That must be a terrific feeling, to know that you're where you were meant to be."

"I've been there a couple of times in my life," he said. "But being there and staying there aren't the same thing. That's why when it's sweet, you savor it, and when it grows sour, you spit it out and move on. Cowboy philosophy," he said, causally dismissing his bit of insight.

"Perhaps I'll adopt it."

"The snow's starting to fall harder. We should probably head back to the house."

They took a shortcut to the stables, this time with Jack's horse taking the lead. Kelly helped him with the horses and then they walked back to the house together.

"I'll make some hot chocolate," Jack said, "and build a fire."

"Sounds good." Kelly went to her room to change into a pair of comfortable sweats, but she never got her hot chocolate. She stretched across the bed for what she'd planned to be only a minute and fell sound asleep.

Monday, 9:15 p.m.
Single S Ranch

KELLY WOKE TO DARKNESS, and it took her a second to remember where she was and that it had been late afternoon when she'd fallen across the bed. The wind whistled and howled like angry ghosts. Kelly slid out of bed and walked to the window to stare out at the driving snow. The blizzard had arrived.

She tried to switch on the lamp, but there was no response. She hadn't expected they'd lose power so soon—unless it was later than she thought. Without bothering to find her slippers in the dark, she padded into the den in her stocking feet. The fire was blazing, embers dancing up the chimney like fireflies.

Jack was stretched out on the couch, his legs and feet wrapped in a striped Indian blanket. "Why didn't you wake me?" she asked.

"You haven't had much sleep over the last few days and there was nothing to wake you for except to watch the snow."

He sat up to make room for her to sit beside him, but she stayed and warmed herself by the fire. "I should call and check on Alex."

"Alex is fine. I talked to her a few minutes ago. You might want to check with your mother, though. She's called three times. I think she fears I'll ravish you now that the two of us are alone."

Kelly stood by the fire, looking at Jack, as masculine as his cabin, yet easy and warm. Dynamic and heroic when he needed to be, yet never pushy or vain. And always incredibly sexy.

"Ravish me, Jack. Ravish me here, on the floor in front of the fire. Take me back to Canyon Road."

He was silent for much too long. Finally he took a deep breath and exhaled slowly. "I can't do that."

The unexpected rejection hurt.

He walked over to her and raked his fingers through her tousled hair. Tucking a thumb beneath her chin, he tilted her face upward so that she had to meet his penetrating gaze. "There's no way to return to Canyon Road. We've both traveled too far to go back."

"Then make love to me here, in this place."

He put both hands on her shoulders, then let his fingers trail her arms until their hands clasped. "Is this about me, Kelly, or is it about hating Nick?"

She ached to tell him it was just about him, but how could she be sure? How could she know for certain that anything she felt wasn't a reaction to the fear and the stress and the fury of the last few days?

"I made a big pot of chili," he said, leading her away from the fire and toward the kitchen where gas lanterns cast a golden glow on the old linoleum and the stained oak table. "You must be starved."

Tuesday, 12:30 a.m.
Single S Ranch

JACK TOSSED RESTLESSLY, alone in his old iron bed. Kelly was only steps down the hall. Turning away from her tonight had been the hardest thing he'd ever done. He wanted her. God, how he wanted her. Before tonight, he would have bet the ranch that given the chance he would have made love with her on any terms. But when it had come right down to it, he knew he wanted more.

He hadn't been looking for promises of everlasting love. He wasn't that much a dreamer anymore. But he'd waited too long for this. When he made love with Kelly he needed it to be about desire and passion and not just a release for her fury.

Still, he ached for her. And he knew sleep would be a long time in coming. He'd finally closed his eyes when he heard Kelly's footfalls in the hallway. His door creaked open.

"Are you awake?" Kelly whispered.

"Yeah."

"I've had time to think about your question."

"And?"

"The fury and resentment's about Nick. The horse ride was about release. But the passion is all about you."

Chapter Thirteen

Tuesday, 12:58 a.m.
Single S Ranch

Kelly shed the sherbet robe at the foot of Jack's bed and stood there for breathtaking seconds, her nude body shimmering in the silvery reflection from the snow outside his window. It was the dream that had haunted him for almost half his life.

But this time it was real. He made a place for her next to him and she crawled beneath the cotton quilt and fit herself into his waiting arms. He touched her tentatively, as if she were still a dream that would shatter if he made the wrong move.

There was no such hesitancy on Kelly's part. She initiated the first kiss, taking his lips hungrily and invading his mouth with her tongue. And then passion took hold and the wanton hunger he'd nursed for so long took on a life of its own.

He kissed her mouth, her cheeks, her eyes, and

then trailed tiny kisses along the curve of her neck. He wanted to go slowly, to savor every inch of her, but his hunger for her was all consuming, driving him to devour all of her at once.

Kelly's hands roamed his back, pressing here and there and sliding down to curl about his buttocks. Without inhibition, she helped him wiggle out of his boxer shorts, finally snagging them with her toe and yanking them past his feet.

The heat between them was like steam, and they kicked back the covers in unison as he raised to straddle her beautiful body. She writhed beneath him and her nipples grew erect and pebbled as he brushed them with his thumbs and then his lips.

In bed, like everywhere else, she responded so openly that he knew immediately what excited her, and exciting her excited him.

"Kelly. Sweet, sweet Kelly." He crooned the words as he kissed and sucked one nipple, then the other, his erection throbbing and pulsing against her soft flesh.

"Oh, Jack. That feels so good. You feel so good." She moved so that she could slip her hands between them and tease the tip of his hardness with quick feathery caresses that almost drove him over the edge.

"I want you inside me, Jack," she whispered. "I want to feel that thrust when you make us one."

"I won't be able to last long."

"It's okay. I'm ready. I am so ready. I think I've always been." She took his hand and guided his fingers to the hot, slick dampness that pooled between her legs.

He wanted to linger there, to taste the salty sweetness of her hot juices, wanted to pleasure her over and over until she cried out in the ecstasy of surrender.

But one of her hands had wrapped around his erection while the other circled and explored, mixing her wetness with his. I need you, Jack. I need all of you. So deep inside me." She slipped a finger between his lips, wanting him to taste her, yet begging him to enter.

He couldn't hold back, so he lifted his hips and let her guide him inside her. She moaned softly, and her body tightened around him.

"Oh, Jack." She half sang, half moaned his name, and his heart felt as if it were going to fracture into a million pieces.

He tried to hold back. He'd waited so long. But the blood rush took over and he could no more stop than he could have stopped loving her.

"Kelly, I…" The passion swallowed his words. They were rocking together, harder and harder, faster and faster, soaring to a crescendo and climaxing in an eruption that seemed to tear him apart. He moaned and fell back to the bed, so physically and emotionally drained, he couldn't breathe or speak.

It was not that way for Kelly. She kissed him again, a quick hot meeting of their lips and merging of their breaths before she snuggled against him.

"Was it Canyon Road?" she whispered.

"No. No way." He let his face burrow in the silky

strands of her hair. "That night was fantastic, the kind of night you remember the rest of your life."

He kissed the back of her neck and then put his mouth to her ear. "Tonight was a hundred times better in every way."

Tuesday, 2:30 p.m.
Single S Ranch

KELLY HAD FALLEN ASLEEP in Jack's arms last night, fulfilled in ways she'd forgotten were possible. Jack had not only satisfied her physical cravings, but had made her feel sexy and seductive.

The afterglow had still been warm inside her when Jack's body had stirred again. The second time they took it slower, and he'd kissed, fondled and sucked every erogenous zone of her body and given her time to do the same for him.

It had been a sensual dance of exploration and she'd not only learned about his body but discovered new and erotic things about her own. Jack was an excellent teacher.

The best discovery of all had been that the titillating, glorious, heart-stopping magic of Canyon Road and the first time she'd ever made love was still alive and well. A magic that she'd never felt with anyone else in all her thirty-two years.

So much for Hollywood.

Unfortunately, she couldn't stay here in this magical world. She had to go back to Beverly Hills and work through all the legal issues and find a way to deal with the millions of dollars of debt Nick had bequeathed her.

And she had to tell Alex that her father had been murdered in Denver. That's all she'd tell her now. Then somehow, when she was older, Kelly would concoct a story that painted Nick in the best light possible, giving Alex only the barest of facts before she heard them from someone else.

Kelly looked back to the notes she'd been making before erotic thoughts of Jack had broken her concentration.

She'd talked to Nick's accountant a few minutes ago. He was firmly convinced that Nick didn't have any bank accounts other than the three she already knew about, but then he was unaware that Nick had sold the property in Mexico. Obviously, Nick hadn't run all his business through the accounting firm so who knew what else he might have been into.

She'd also made a call to her attorney, but had only talked to him briefly as he'd been on his way to court. He was going to contact Nick's attorney and try to facilitate the reading and interpretation of the will so that she'd know exactly where she stood.

Among other things, he'd instructed her that in the meantime she should live in the house to preserve the integrity of her rights and to keep the property and its furnishings intact. Lawyers had such a way with words. She wondered if they took classes in legal jargon the way she'd taken French and Spanish at UCLA.

Bottom line: It was goodbye Jack, hello Beverly Hills. She got cold chills just thinking about walking back into the house that had Nick Warner's ghost lurking in every corner.

Jack walked in from the kitchen where he'd been on the phone with Lenny for the last half hour.

"Any news?" she asked.

"Very little. Lenny located a Milo Kardascian who lives in Denver, but couldn't find any connection between him and Nick, or between Milo and Karen. He's a rich businessman with a penchant for beating up girlfriends. He'd filed a suit claiming police brutality, but it looks as if it has little merit."

"He must have had some significance to whatever Karen was investigating."

"You're right. I'll hold on to the name and red flag it in the PPS system. It might make sense one day."

"What about the Puerto Escondido deal?

"No luck yet." He shrugged. "Enough business. Have you talked to Alex?"

"Twice. She's excited about the snow. I talked to my mother, too, about letting Alex fly back home with them and stay for a week while I deal with the legal hassles."

"And she agreed, of course."

"She and Dad were both thrilled. They're going to bring her home on Friday so she can attend her preschool class next week and hopefully return some normalcy to her routine."

"I guess that means you're going back to Beverly Hills."

"Tomorrow. I was just about to ask if I could use your computer to book a flight. Mitchell called and offered again to charter a jet, but I told him we were living in the new age of minimalism and that I was going to fly coach. He was appalled. But not as appalled as he was when I told him he could plan some sort of service for Nick if he liked, but that I would not be attending."

"I take it you told him that Nick hired the hit man?"

"Yes, and he said that Jack Sanders was either experiencing delusions or outright lying, and that he'd known that PPS was nothing more than a high-priced rip-off from the beginning."

Stormy started barking at the door. Nick walked over to let him out, but Stormy changed his mind and just sat there looking woebegone.

"He misses Alex," Jack said.

"And I'm sure she misses him, too. Maybe I should get her a dog when things are more settled."

"She should have Stormy. They've already bonded. I'll deliver him to Beverly Hills when you give me the go-ahead."

He propped his foot on the hearth and stared into the fire. She couldn't see his eyes, but the set of his jaw and the pull to his mouth made her uneasy.

"Is there something you're not telling me?"

He shook his head and offered a poor imitation of a smile.

"You don't think this is over, do you, Jack? You're waiting for the other shoe to drop."

"I'm just not ready for you to go."

She didn't totally buy that, but then she knew he'd talked to Evangeline that morning. He could already have his next assignment on his mind.

"I'll miss you, bodyguard, but I have to go back to Tinseltown. All this fresh air is bad for my lungs."

Finally he dropped to the couch beside her and snaked his arm around her shoulder. "I'll book the flights."

"Flights—as in plural? I can't afford you, Jack. I don't know how I'll pay the PPS bill as it is."

He trailed a few kisses down the back of her neck. "I've asked for a couple of days off and have already cleared it with Evangeline. Besides, I can't very well let you face returning to that house alone."

She tilted her head back and looked him in the eye. "Are you for real, Jack Sanders?"

He took her hand in his and slid it to the growing bulge inside his jeans. "Does that feel real to you?"

No, it was magic. Pure magic.

Wednesday 2:45 p.m.
Beverly Hills

"A LITTLE SHABBY, but it'll do," Jack said, as the taxi they'd taken from the airport pulled through the massive iron gate and started down the tree-lined drive to the Warner estate. It was the first time she'd taken a taxi instead of a limo. Part of the new Kelly.

"Do you share a zip code or have your own?"

"I have my own," she quipped. "In all the zip codes in all the countries in the world, you had to walk into mine."

The teasing failed to relieve the tension that had gripped her ever since they'd stepped off the plane. It wasn't the house; it was what the house represented. She'd spent just over five years of her life playing the role of Mrs. Nick Warner without ever exploring what the pretense was doing to her.

She'd accepted the world of hype and publicity where starlets jumped from bed to bed and marriage licenses were printed in disappearing ink. A world where living separate lives in a house the size of a small village didn't seem particularly unusual.

She'd shopped on Rodeo Drive, sent her daughter to an elite playschool, flown in chartered jets and had a staff to take care of every detail of her life.

It had all been a cop-out. And she was through copping out. Hard as it might be, she was going to take control of her life. No more hiding behind accountants and managers and attorneys. No more playing betrayed little rich girl, either. She'd get the facts, make the decisions and the chips would fall where they may.

The driver opened her door and she stepped out and walked to the entrance. Everything looked exactly the same as when she'd left it a mere six days ago. The front lawn was perfectly manicured. The walk was spotlessly clean. The front doors were gleaming.

Jack stepped beside her, luggage in both hands and swinging from both shoulders.

"It's just a house," he said. "Remember that." She opened the door and he let out a low whistle. "Let me rephrase that. It's just a mansion."

"My suite's through the foyer and at the end of the hallway to your left," she said. "Just follow me."

"If I get lost, send the dogs to find me."

"No dogs. No cats. Nick was allergic to animal hair."

"Are we the only ones here? No servants?"

"Nick gave the household crew a week off while we were in Denver. He probably wanted them rested so they could take good care of him while he mourned." And just the thought stirred her fury and hurt and set her stomach churning.

She opened the door to her suite and almost jumped out of her skin. "Mitchell, what are doing in here?"

"I could tell how upset you were yesterday when we talked and I thought I should be here to welcome you home." He nonchalantly went back to putting the final touches on a large crystal vase of yellow roses. "I thought the flowers in your sitting room might help your mood."

"That was thoughtful." She tossed her handbag onto the love seat by the door. "I thought you were in Denver."

"I flew—" His stopped midsentence as Jack stepped into the room. "What's he doing here?"

"He's here to—" This time it was she who stopped midsentence. She didn't owe Mitchell an explanation. "Jack's my guest.

"I see."

"Good to see you, too, Mitchell," Jack said. "Where should I put the bags, Kelly?"

"In the bedroom for now." She pointed to the open door to her left.

Mitchell walked over and helped her shrug out of her blazer. "I hope Jack's being here doesn't imply that you're still in some kind of danger."

"No. He's flying back to Denver in the morning. Everything's okay."

"Good, I know I've been occupied with my grief for Nick, but I do worry about you, too."

"I understand." He was still convinced of Nick's innocence in all of this, and she really did have to cut him some slack.

"I'll be fine, Mitchell. I have plenty to keep me busy until Alex and my parents get here this weekend."

"Then I guess I should be going?"

"I didn't see your car when we drove up."

"I parked in the back, and I'll let myself out so you can get back to Jack."

"You take care," she said, "and thanks again for the flowers."

She walked to the bedroom where Jack was standing at her sliding-glass door watching the gardener replace potted plants around the pool with ones that were blooming profusely.

"That was interesting," Jack said.

"Nick liked the potted plants changed on a regular basis."

"No, I meant Mitchell. Does he always let himself in and out of your house like that?"

"Everyone lets themselves in and out of this house. Nick had a swinging-door policy."

"That didn't give you and Alex much privacy."

"His friends never came to my end of the hall, and I never went to Nick's suite in the east wing. I'll give you a grand tour of the house later. First I think we should have lunch."

"Then I find a hardware store and buy and install all new locks for the house. After that, the tour."

"I can call a locksmith for that."

"A locksmith? Have you forgotten who you're talking to?"

"Excuse me, Mr. Surveillance Expert, by all means, you take care of the locks. Now let's go see if I find my way around my own kitchen while you check out the wine closet."

She started toward the kitchen. Jack didn't follow. "Do you know that you have a camera over your bed?"

"We didn't put it there. It must have been installed by the people who lived here before us."

Jack kicked out of his shoes and climbed onto the bed, reaching up to unscrew a bronze inset from the fan. "This was installed recently. It's the latest in technology. You program it for the times you want it to take pictures. This particular model takes up to five hundred pictures before you have to change the film."

"How do you know all that?"

"I used this exact camera on a case last month."

Kelly watched over his shoulder as he flicked through a series of digital pictures. Some were just of the empty room, but many were of her in various stages of undress."

"I don't understand. Nick was gay. Why would he have kept something like this in my bedroom."

"It may not have been Nick."

She shuddered and her stomach took a sickening turn. "Lunch and then locks," she said. But she'd completely lost her appetite.

Wednesday, 5:20 p.m.
Beverly Hills

AS FAR AS JACK was concerned, the most reassuring news of the day had come from Gilly Carter. They already had a preliminary ballistics report back—amazing how fast they could get results when a celebrity and the national news media were involved. The gun Kelly had found in Hal's hotel room was the weapon used to kill Nick.

There really was no valid, professional reason for him to stay on here with Kelly, but he wouldn't leave until he knew the house was secure and that the alarm system was functioning properly.

Jack had spent the afternoon changing out the

locks and searching for hidden surveillance equipment. He'd only found one other camera, and that had been placed so that it gave a full view of Kelly's bath and dressing area.

Some perverted voyeur had been getting his jollies spying on Kelly, and now she had to deal with feeling violated on top of everything else.

He finished checking the living area and stopped at the double winding staircase. "What's upstairs?"

"Mostly storage. The big room to the left is what I refer to as Party Central. Nick's parties were famous even by Beverly Hills standards, especially his Halloween and Valentine's Day events."

"Anything besides storage?"

"Nick made one of the rooms into an office last fall. I couldn't say what he does in it or what it looks like. I've never been in it."

"Then I'll just take a quick look around."

He passed and saluted a life-size Roman soldier at the landing. The sculpture looked as if it weighed a ton and would have been more at home in a museum.

Once up the stairs, Jack hit Party Central first. It was like something from a B-movie horror film with ghosts and ghouls and even a very real-looking dummy with a noose around its limp neck, hanging from a meat hook.

The Valentine's Day decorations were not much cheerier. They ranged from funny to mildly deviant to sickeningly aberrant.

Jack didn't stay in there long or in the other

rooms, most used for storage, just as Kelly had said. There was only one room left, so it had to be Nick's office. Jack opened the door and stepped inside. The desk was cluttered with scribbled notes and printed pages that looked to be a manuscript of some kind.

The wall behind the desk was lined with posters from Nick's movies. Jack turned to check out the rest of the room, then stopped to stare at a grouping of pictures that sent a few pangs right down to his gut.

He'd pegged Nick Warner wrong.

Chapter Fourteen

The display of photographs took up about half the wall. The frames were a mismatched combination of colors, styles and sizes, the only thing in the entire house that looked as if it hadn't seen a decorator's hand. The subject was the only thing that remained constant.

Every photograph was of Alex, most of her alone, though some included Nick.

Alex in her high chair with chocolate cupcake smeared all over her hands and face.

Alex pushing a doll stroller.

Alex on a carousel horse with a huge smile on her face.

Alex with a wad of cotton candy in her mouth.

Alex as a toddler, sitting on Nick's stomach and feeding him a bite of her cookie.

The typical pictures a loving father would cherish.

This was the Nick that Kelly had described to Jack—
a man with a multitude of faults, but a man who
adored his daughter.

Jack propped his backside against Nick's desk,
troubled, yet mesmerized by one picture in particular. It was a snapshot of Alex as a newborn cradled
in Nick's arms, and the look on his face was pure
adulation.

No wonder it had been so difficult for Kelly to
believe Nick capable of sacrificing his daughter even
for a three-million-dollar payoff. But then who knew
what was really going on in his mind or what kind
of trouble he might have gotten into?

Jack had a feeling that they had only scratched the
surface of what had been behind Nick's decision, but
he was almost certain now that it would be more than
just the influence of Hal Hayden.

Thursday, 8:08 a.m.
Beverly Hills

KELLY STEPPED OUT of the shower and immediately
covered up in the fluffy white towel. Even shower-
ing in this house had become a disgusting experi-
ence. There were no cameras in here now, but she felt
as if a hundred dirty, perverted eyes were on her.

The confidence she'd tried to exude yesterday
morning had taken a nosedive. She'd dreaded coming back to this house, but being here was far more
difficult than she'd imagined. Even Jack was differ-

ent here. He'd been incredibly understanding of how
severely the pictures on the cameras had upset her.
Still, he'd hardly talked during dinner and he'd
tossed and turned all night. She wasn't sure if he'd
ever fallen asleep.

He was at the computer in the housekeeping office
just off the kitchen now, scrolling computerized PPS
files and drinking coffee, already dressed for his
eleven o'clock flight. He was so preoccupied that
he'd barely looked up when she'd found him and
kissed him good-morning.

Kelly slipped into a lilac silk robe. Jack was used
to eating breakfast and she had to go and see if her
hand still fit a skillet.

Thursday, 8:42 a.m.
Beverly Hills

KELLY SAT AT the kitchen table, taking advantage of
the fact that the household staff was still on vacation.
The creditor spreadsheet that Lenny had just faxed
over was propped in front of her, but it was so overwhelming she didn't know where to start.

Always best to use a proven method in decision
making, so she closed her eyes, circled the pen a few
times like a plane coming in for landing, then
lowered the point to…

She opened her eyes. Ugh. She'd landed on the
credit card section, the largest section of all. Going
through these would keep her busy until bedtime.

She dialed the 800 number for the first listing, thankful that Lenny had provided not only phone numbers but Nick's account numbers, as well. A computerized voice instructed her to punch four for assistance with account inquiries. An operator answered promptly then put her on hold.

Kelly stared out the kitchen window. There was a nice view of the garden. But no snow. No horses. No Jack. She missed him already, and he wasn't even at LAX yet.

"This call may be monitored for…"

Yada, yada, yada, let's get on with it. She supplied the basic answers and finally got to make her simple request. "My husband died last week and I can't find any statements from you. I think he may have—"

"One moment, please, while I switch you to bookkeeping."

Here she went again. Five minutes later, she seemed to be on a roll.

"How may I help you, Mrs. Warner?"

Kelly explained the situation again. "I'm thinking that my husband must have used some kind of online paperless billing because I can't find current or past statements. I'd like to have copies of the last twelve months' purchases."

If she was going to pay, she was going to know what she was paying for and have an accurate record of what had been paid.

"No, the statements are mailed directly to you every month."

"At what address?"

The woman read off an address in Beverly Hills; it wasn't theirs.

"Are you certain that's where the statements are mailed?"

"Yes, ma'am, but you can do a change of address. You'll just have to send it in writing…."

Kelly didn't listen to the rest of the spiel. Instead she called the next number on the list, and the next and the next before moving to car dealerships.

The result was always the same. Statements were mailed directly to Mitchell Caruthers's address. He'd said he knew nothing of the state of Nick's finances.

He'd lied. She intended to find out why.

Thursday, 11:40 a.m.
Beverly Hills

KELLY HEARD A KNOCK at her back door. Startled, she rushed for a look out the peephole. Mitchell. Just the man she wanted to see. Kelly turned the deadbolt and opened the door. She spotted his car parked near their four-vehicle garage. "Looks as if you have a new car, Mitchell. That's an Aston Martin, isn't it?"

"Yes, and it rides beautifully."

"Did Nick buy that for you? I notice he owes their financing department a few hundred thousand dollars for one."

"He did give it to me. You know how generous he

was, but he told me he paid cash. I would never have accepted it otherwise."

"Really."

Kelly could feel her blood pressure rising. No wonder he was so heavy into grief. His gravy train had derailed. It would be nice to know just how much of the amount owed on those endless charge accounts had gone for things that had wound up on Mitchell's body, in his house, or parked in his garage. Who would have known, with all the bills being routed through him?

Her phone rang. She would have ignored it, but she needed a minute to think how she should handle the confrontation with Mitchell. Too bad she couldn't ask Jack but he was somewhere in the air between here and Denver.

"Hello."

"Hey, kid. It's Drake. When did you get back?"

"Yesterday."

"Did you find the flowers I brought by."

"No. Where did you leave them?

"I put them in your sitting room so you'd be sure to see them when you got home. There was a card."

"How did you get in?"

"With the key you gave me the day you wanted me to pick up Alex and bring her with me to cut that video. Don't you remember?"

"I do now."

"I hope you don't mind that I took them inside. I expected the housekeeper to be there, but no one answered the door and I didn't want to leave them just sitting around."

"Maybe I did see them and just missed the card. Yellow roses?"

"Yeah, the old standby. You know me. I'm not imaginative when it comes to flowers."

So Mitchell had even taken credit for the flowers that were in her sitting room—where he had no right to be. So why had he been in there? Surely not— Her skin crawled at the thought.

He lied blatantly. He took advantage of every opportunity. Perhaps he'd even been stealing from Nick's accounts. So why wouldn't he stoop so low as to put hidden cameras in her bed and bath? He could always use them for blackmail purposes or sell them on the Internet. Or just use them for his own dirty fantasies. Mitchell wasn't gay.

He would have had plenty of opportunity, but she had no proof it was him. She'd have to wait to talk to Jack. He'd know how to handle this. But in the meantime, she had to get rid of Mitchell.

She started back to the kitchen, but Mitchell was waiting for her in the doorway. The blade of a butcher's knife gleamed in his hand and he was smiling and moving his fingers back and forth along the dull edge of the blade as if he were—

Oh, my, God! He was going to kill her.

Adrenaline rushed through her bloodstream. She had to get out of the house, but she couldn't get to the back door without running by him. Impulsively, she grabbed a heavy crystal bowl from the counter and hurled it at him. It missed his head, but crashed into his chest.

The impact knocked him backward, giving her a second to bolt thorough the door that led into the huge foyer. She was still fumbling with the double dead bolts on the front door when Mitchell's hand closed on her arm.

"You couldn't leave well enough alone, could…"

She bit hard into the flesh of his forearm, tasting blood through his shirt. His grip loosened, and she swung her elbows into his already-wounded chest and took off running again.

This time she took the staircase, her breath burning as she neared the landing. She didn't turn, but she knew he was only steps behind her. She heard his panting and curses and the pounding of his feet.

If she could only make it to the landing, she could shove Nick's Italian sculpture into his path and slow him down. She was inches away from it when Mitchell grabbed her right foot and yanked her to the floor.

She clawed at the carpet with one hand and grabbed for a baluster with the other as he dragged her down the staircase. But Mitchell was too strong. And then he stopped pulling and she felt the knife digging into her wrist. He was going to slice her veins. Why the hell did everyone want her dead?

Desperation and fury sent a new wave of adrenaline rushing though her. She kicked hard with her foot, catching Mitchell in the knee. He went to the floor behind her and the knife slipped from his hand.

The second it took him to retrieve it was all she needed to reach the landing. It took all her strength and precious seconds to topple the heavy statue, but she did it. It crashed into the balustrade, sending splintered wood raining down on them.

She grabbed one sharp piece and started running again.

Mitchell had somehow dodged the tumbling statue, but one of the splintered pieces of wood had punctured his leg like an arrow. He shouted curses as he pulled it out, but she was on the second floor now. The only escape would be a twenty-foot drop from a window to the ground. She'd have to jump.

She darted into Party Central, not slowing to close the door behind her as she rushed to the window. She unlocked it and tried to shove it upward. It didn't budge.

She banged on the facing, rattling the pane. She tried it again, but it stuck tight. She could break out one of the panes of glass, but the squares were so small she'd never be able to squeeze through.

She looked back to the door. Mitchell was standing just inside it, blood pouring from his leg, but the knife still clutched in his hand.

She fell to the floor and started crawling between the clusters of decorations, but it was futile. There was nowhere to go where he couldn't reach her. And even her sliver of splintered wood was back by the window.

She hovered behind a metal Cupid who smiled at

her sardonically. She heard the phone ringing. And then she felt the blade of the knife, only this time it was at her throat.

"Why? Why kill me? Just tell me why?"

"Your husband was an idiot. He was going to throw away everything I'd worked for with his drinking and carousing all night, every night. The studio was going to drop him."

"That was him, not me."

"But the insurance policy is on you. And now you've messed up my plans again. Suicide would have been nicer on all of us. A quick slice of your wrists in the kitchen. But now you've wrecked the house, so it will have to look as if the hitman Nick hired to kill you honored his contract in spite of everything."

"No one will believe that."

"But I'll see that they do. I still have a note with the hitman's fingerprints on it to leave on the steps where you tried bravely, but futilely, to fight him off."

"It was you, not Hal. You killed Nick, and you paid someone to kill me—and Alex if it came to that."

Mitchell laughed, and she could feel the first prick of the knife cutting into her flesh.

She was going to die here among the ghoulish creatures. She wouldn't be there to see Alex off for her first day of school, or wear her first prom dress, or walk the aisle in a snow-white wedding gown.

And she'd never told Jack she loved him or thanked him for the magic.

Chapter Fifteen

Jack had figured it wrong, and it might have stayed wrong if he hadn't been so troubled by the pictures in Nick's office. He'd thought about it all night, went over a thousand different scenarios in his mind.

And then it all started coming together at the airport, just before his flight, when he'd surfed and found a flyer Hal Hayden had circulated on the Internet last year. Anything for a price, accompanied by a picture of him in a loincloth.

Lenny had added vital new information when he'd discovered that Mitchell, not Nick, had flown to Puerto Escondido the day of the sale and then on to the Cayman Islands where he'd deposited two million dollars in an account that he'd opened just after Nick's first big film.

The way Jack saw it, Mitchell had hired Hal to

seduce Nick and set up his whole murderous scheme. He didn't have it all figured out yet, but it didn't look good for Mitchell Caruthers.

"The gate's just ahead," Jack told the taxi driver. "On the left, and hit the accelerator."

"Settle down, bud. It's L.A. We've got speed limits and traffic. You wanna get here sooner, you start out sooner."

Jack tried Kelly's cell phone number again. Still no answer. No answer on her house phone, either.

So where the hell was she?

No reason for panic. Mitchell couldn't know that his sordid plot had been uncovered. And he wouldn't risk hiring another hit man so soon, not after he'd played the game so brilliantly to this point.

No reason to panic, but dread was knocking around inside him all the same. Jack didn't wait for the taxi to come to a stop before he tossed a couple of twenties into the front seat and jumped from the vehicle.

The spare keys to the locks he'd installed yesterday were in his hand by the time he reached the door. He unlocked it quickly and pushed into the foyer.

"Kelly! *Kelly!*"

He yelled her name, and then he saw the head of the Roman soldier rolling around on the floor near the mangled staircase. Terror exploded in his chest and he leaped over the chipped and headless soldier and raced up the staircase.

He couldn't lose Kelly. Not this way. Not now!

The door to Party Central was open.

Gun drawn and his finger on the trigger, Jack peered inside. There was no sign of Kelly or Mitchell, only rows of grotesque faces taunting him.

He worked his way through the maze of ghouls, pausing when he stepped into a trickle of blood.

His heart stopped beating for one excruciating second.

"I'm over here, Jack."

He looked toward the sound of her voice, and saw her crumpled against the wall. Blood dripped down the front of her white shirt and soaked the waist of her skirt. Alert for any sign of Mitchell, he fell to her side and cradled her in his arms as he checked her pulse. It was much too fast, as if her heart were racing.

"I'll call an ambulance," Jack said. "We'll get you to the hospital."

"No. I'm okay."

"You're covered in blood."

"It's Mitchell's blood. I think I killed him, Jack." Her voice was scratchy and barely a whisper. "Over there, behind the red heart."

He got up and walked over to kick the blow-up heart aside. Mitchell was still half hidden by a metal Cupid who'd lost his weapon. The missing arrow had gone in through Mitchell's back and out through his side.

He was bleeding profusely—but not dead. Jack saw the clinch in his jaw and caught the glint of the blade of a knife. He lunged at Mitchell just as he raised himself enough to hurl the knife at Kelly.

Jack grabbed his arm in time to foil his aim. The knife missed its mark and plunged into the wall just inches from Kelly's head. Mitchell coughed, spitting up blood before bellowing a string of vile curses.

"He killed Nick," Kelly said, her voice stronger and steadier. "He was gong to kill me."

"I know. I should have been here. I should have been with you."

"You were," she said, standing, but still leaning against the wall. "You called my name and when Mitchell turned, I grabbed the arrow and struck him with all my might. I couldn't let him kill you, too."

Jack made a quick call to 911, then, his gun pointed at the groaning and cursing Mitchell Caruthers, he gathered Kelly in his arms and held her tight.

He wasn't exactly sure what had happened, but the details could wait. Right now all he knew was that he'd come much too close to losing Kelly and that life without her wouldn't be life at all.

Epilogue

Jack hung up the phone from a conference call with a chain of local convenience stores that was upgrading its surveillance systems after a string of recent robberies. He glanced at his watch for at least the tenth time in the last half hour.

He was picking Kelly up at the airport at four-thirty, and he didn't want to be late. They'd talked on the phone every day since he'd flown back to Denver, but this would be the first time they'd been together.

He looked up as Cameron popped into his cubicle and straddled a chair.

"Whew! This place is hopping," Cameron said. "I think all the agents are knee-deep in work."

"Good for job security." Jack glanced at his watch. "Though I don't want any new assignments this afternoon."

"That's right, Kelly's flying in today, isn't she? Are you nervous?"

"Me, nervous?"

"Like you get visited by a hot California babe every day. And there was some definite chemistry clicking between you two. How'd that case finally come down? Was Nick Warner's manager-publicist really the mastermind behind the shebang?"

"It looks that way. He was robbing Nick blind, not living nearly as extravagantly as Nick, but doing well for himself. Plus he was investing a lot of money and stashing some in a bank in the Cayman Islands. The situation's got all the earmarks of a man who thought he might have to make a quick exodus out of the country soon. We may never know that whole story."

"The paper says he's admitting everything."

"At the insistence of his attorney, I'm sure. But that doesn't mean he won't keep a few secrets," Jack said with a grimace.

"But he was the one who hired a hit man to kill Alex?"

"He put up the money. Hal delivered it to Degrazia, who's also been arrested, thanks to our sharing lots of info with Detective Gilly Carter."

"Who probably never even said thanks. Those detectives do hate to give us credit. So did Billy Sheffield lie about seeing Nick Warner in the limo?" Cameron asked.

"No, Nick was there. They'd flown over together for some prefestival publicity with the Chamber of

Commerce. Hal was to pretend they were lost and that he was asking for directions when he made the payoff, then make sure Nick put down the window and waved to one of his *big fans* as they drove off. Nick was a man of the people—among other things."

"But Nick jumped the gun and put down the window on his own with Billy, if I remember that right."

"That's how it went down."

"And they couldn't hire a hit man to kill Nick because they'd set him up to be the one doing the hiring. So, was Nick's death supposed to look like an attack by the stalker who broke into the house?" Cameron queried.

"Right. The police found all kinds of notes in Nick's house from a man claiming he was going to kill him for cheating on Kelly. Mitchell admitted sending those, too."

"Gotta hand it to him. He didn't miss a trick."

"Very disciplined, and not a bad actor, either."

"So who did break into the rented house and shoot that guard?"

"Hal, again. Killed the guard with the same gun he used to kill Nick, all proven by the ballistics report."

"What a web. Do you think Hal actually fell off that balcony?"

"Not a chance. Mitchell pushed him, but he's never going to admit that. As it stands now, he hasn't actually killed anybody. I'm sure his high-priced defense attorney is going to push that fact along with Mitchell's willingness to cooperate and his remorse—which he's playing up big-time.

"Guess all's well that ends well."

"I have a hunch that the tale of Mitchell Caruthers and Nick Warner may not be totally over."

"What makes you think that?"

"A few nagging, unanswered questions."

"Such as?"

"The reason Karen Butte was so desperate to see Kelly the night before she was murdered and then there was that name she text messaged me that doesn't seem connected to anything." Jack glanced at his watch again. "Gotta run."

"Right, Mr. Not Nervous. Have a great weekend."

"Giving it my best shot." Jack grabbed his briefcase and headed toward the door. He had one stop to make on the way to the airport, a little gift for Kelly, if he got up the nerve to give it to her.

He was nervous as hell, planning to put his emotions right out there on his sleeve for the very first time. It was risky, but a chance he had to take.

He gave Angel a nod as he rushed past her desk.

"Is this for you?" she asked, holding up a disk and waving it at him.

"Was it addressed to me?"

"No, just to PPS, so I don't know what to do with it."

"Who's it from?"

She picked up a brown envelope and looked. "No return address."

"Then give it to anybody but me. I'm out of here."

IT WAS NO CANYON ROAD, but the fire was blazing and he'd bought real crystal stems for the wine. He poured them each a glass and joined Kelly in the den where she was sitting on the floor and renewing her friendship with Stormy.

"Wow! Crystal. I'm impressed." She jumped up to take a glass.

"If that excites you, wait till you taste my steak."

"Aww. I had my taste buds all set for your chili."

"Tomorrow night."

She held up her glass. "What shall we drink to?"

"To a great weekend."

"To a magical weekend," she corrected. She clinked her glass with his, then curled up on the couch. He sat down on the other end, feeling tense and awkward, afraid the night would not go well.

She turned so that they were facing each other. "It's good to be here. It seems I've been away forever."

"You've had a lot of changes in you life since you were here last."

"I feel as if I'm in a constant state of flux. Mom and Dad have helped a lot. Dad raves about you all the time, by the way. You're the hero who saved his daughter."

"I've come a long way."

"Yes you have, Jack Sanders. Alex talks about you, too. And Stormy, and Pete and Repeat, and Ishwar. I didn't tell her I was coming here this weekend. She'd have wanted to come."

"How is she?"

Kelly stared into the fire, showing her first sign

of melancholy. "Most of the time she's fine, but sometimes it's hard for her. She can't quite grasp that Nick's never coming back, but then she was used to his being away a lot on location or vacations, and I think that might be part of the confusion. I'm just thankful that I could honestly tell her that he loved her very much."

"It's probably good for her that your Mom and Dad are staying with you for a while."

"And good for me, especially now that we have a buyer for the house. With the money from that, and from selling the furniture and the two million that Mitchell had to return from the land sale in Puerto Escondido, I'm actually in the black again."

"Your life is definitely changing."

"It was past time, even if Nick hadn't been killed." She set her glass on the table when Stormy came in from the bedroom dragging the present. "Is that for me?"

"You don't want to open it now."

"Yes I do, but I can't imagine what's in a box that size." She tugged the gift from Stormy and began to rip the paper away. Perspiration pooled on Jack's brow.

She pulled the sign from the box and stared at it. "Interesting. What is it?"

"You're holding it upside down."

She turned it over. "J & K."

"It's a new sign for the gate."

"You're replacing the Single S?"

"I was thinking it might be a good idea."

She stared at him questioningly. "Is this a proposal?"

He was doing this all wrong. He pulled her into his arms. "I love you, Kelly. I've always loved you. I always will."

"Oh, Jack. I love you, too. I love everything about you, but—"

"No, don't answer yet. I don't expect you to rush into anything. I know it's too soon. I should have waited. I should—"

"I need some time—for Alex. Fall weddings are nice." She kissed him, a sweet, passionate kiss that stole his breath. And then she pulled away.

"Go get the nails," she ordered.

"What?"

"Go get the nails and a hammer. We've got a sign to hang."

* * * * *

BODYGUARDS UNLIMITED,
DENVER, COLORADO
continues next month.
Don't miss SPECIAL ASSIGNMENT by
reader favorite Ann Voss Peterson!

Turn the page for a sneak preview of
IF I'D NEVER KNOWN YOUR LOVE
by
Georgia Bockoven

From the brand-new series
HARLEQUIN EVERLASTING LOVE
Every great love has a story to tell. ™

One year, five months and four days missing

There's no way for you to know this, Evan, but I haven't written to you for a few months. Actually, it's been almost a year. I had a hard time picking up a pen once more after we paid the second ransom and then received a letter saying it wasn't enough. I was so sure you were coming home that I took the kids along to Bogotá so they could fly home with you and me, something I swore I'd never do. I've fallen in love with Colombia and the people who've opened their hearts to me. But fear is a constant companion when I'm there. I won't ever expose our children to that kind of danger again.

I'm at a loss over what to do anymore, Evan. I've begged and pleaded and thrown temper tantrums with every official I can corner both here and at home. They've been incredibly tolerant and understanding, but in the end as ineffectual as the rest of us.

I try to imagine what your life is like now, what you do every day, what you're wearing, what you eat. I want to believe that the people who have you are misguided yet kind, that they treat you well. It's how I survive day to day. To think of you being mistreated hurts too much. If I picture you locked away somewhere and suffering, a weight descends on me that makes it almost impossible to get out of bed in the morning.

Your captors surely know you by now. They have to recognize what a good man you are. I imagine you working with their children, telling them that you have children, too, showing them the pictures you carry in your wallet. Can't the men who have you understand how much your children miss you? How can it not matter to them?

How can they keep you away from us all this time? Over and over, we've done what they asked. Are they oblivious to the depth of their cruelty? What kind of people are they that they don't care?

I used to keep a calendar beside our bed next to the peach rose you picked for me before you left. Every night I marked another day, counting how many you'd been gone. I don't do that any longer. I don't want to be reminded of all the days we'll never get back.

When I can't sleep at night, I tell you about my day. I imagine you hearing me and smiling over the details that make up my life now. I never tell you how defeated I feel at moments or how hard I work to hide it from everyone for fear they will see it as a reason to stop believing you are coming home to us.

And I couldn't tell you about the lump I found in my breast and how difficult it was going through all the tests without you here to lean on. The lump was benign—the process reaching that diagnosis utterly terrifying. I couldn't stop thinking about what would happen to Shelly and Jason if something happened to me.

We need you to come home.

I'm worn down with missing you.

I'm going to read this tomorrow and will probably tear it up or burn it in the fireplace. I don't want you to get the idea I ever doubted what I was doing to free you or thought the work a burden. I would gladly spend the rest of my life at it, even if, in the end, we only had one day together.

You are my life, Evan.

I will love you forever.

* * * * *

Don't miss this deeply moving
Harlequin Everlasting Love story
about a woman's struggle to bring back
her kidnapped husband from Colombia and her
turmoil over whether to let go, finally, and
welcome another man into her life.

IF I'D NEVER KNOWN YOUR LOVE
by Georgia Bockoven
is available March 27, 2007.

And also look for
THE NIGHT WE MET
by Tara Taylor Quinn,
a story about finding love
when you least expect it.

HARLEQUIN® *Romance*®

presents a brand-new trilogy by

PATRICIA THAYER

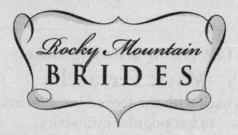

Rocky Mountain
BRIDES

Three sisters come home to wed.

In April don't miss
Raising the Rancher's Family,

followed by

The Sheriff's Pregnant Wife,

on sale May 2007,

and

A Mother for the Tycoon's Child,

on sale June 2007.

www.eHarlequin.com   HRMAR07

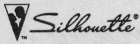

REQUEST YOUR FREE BOOKS!

2 FREE NOVELS PLUS 2 FREE GIFTS!

HARLEQUIN®

INTRIGUE®

Breathtaking Romantic Suspense

YES! Please send me 2 FREE Harlequin Intrigue® novels and my 2 FREE gifts. After receiving them, if I don't wish to receive any more books, I can return the shipping statement marked "cancel." If I don't cancel, I will receive 6 brand-new novels every month and be billed just $4.24 per book in the U.S., or $4.99 per book in Canada, plus 25¢ shipping and handling per book and applicable taxes, if any*. That's a savings of close to 15% off the cover price! I understand that accepting the 2 free books and gifts places me under no obligation to buy anything. I can always return a shipment and cancel at any time. Even if I never buy another book from Harlequin, the two free books and gifts are mine to keep forever.

182 HDN EEZ7 382 HDN EEZK

Name _____ (PLEASE PRINT) _____

Address _____ Apt. # _____

City _____ State/Prov. _____ Zip/Postal Code _____

Signature (if under 18, a parent or guardian must sign)

Mail to the **Harlequin Reader Service®**:
IN U.S.A.: P.O. Box 1867, Buffalo, NY 14240-1867
IN CANADA: P.O. Box 609, Fort Erie, Ontario L2A 5X3

Not valid to current Harlequin Intrigue subscribers.

Want to try two free books from another line?
Call 1-800-873-8635 or visit www.morefreebooks.com.

* Terms and prices subject to change without notice. NY residents add applicable sales tax. Canadian residents will be charged applicable provincial taxes and GST. This offer is limited to one order per household. All orders subject to approval. Credit or debit balances in a customer's account(s) may be offset by any other outstanding balance owed by or to the customer. Please allow 4 to 6 weeks for delivery.

Your Privacy: Harlequin is committed to protecting your privacy. Our Privacy Policy is available online at www.eHarlequin.com or upon request from the Reader Service. From time to time we make our lists of customers available to reputable firms who may have a product or service of interest to you. If you would prefer we not share your name and address, please check here. ☐

HI07

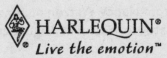

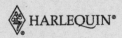

#981 SPECIAL ASSIGNMENT by Ann Voss Peterson
Bodyguards Unlimited, Denver, CO (Book 2 of 6)
Mike Lawson is just the type of honest cop needed to protect
Prescott agent Cassie Allen as police corruption overruns Denver.

#982 PRESCRIPTION: MAKEOVER by Jessica Andersen
In order to expose a vast conspiracy, Ike Rombout undergoes a
full makeover that turns her into exactly the sort of girly-girl she
despises—only to catch the watchful eye of investigator William Caine.

#983 A SOLDIER'S OATH by Debra Webb
Colby Agency: The Equalizers (Book 1 of 3)
Spencer Anders joined the Equalizers to start over. But can he recover
Willow Harris's son from the Middle East *and* give Willow a chance at
a new beginning?

#984 COMPROMISED SECURITY by Cassie Miles
Safe House: Mesa Verde (Book 2 of 2)
FBI special agents Flynn O'Conner and Marisa Kelso must confront
their darkest, most personal secrets while pursuing an elusive killer.

#985 SECRET CONTRACT by Dana Marton
Mission: Redemption (Book 1 of 4)
Undercover soldier Nick Tarasov has been after an untouchable arms
dealer for years, but this time he has Carly Jones with him—and she
has nothing to lose.

#986 FINDING HIS CHILD by Tracy Montoya
Search-and-rescue tracker Sabrina Adelante never gave up looking
for Aaron Donovan's daughter. Aaron still believes his daughter is out
along Renegade Ridge, but is he seeking closure—or vengeance?

www.eHarlequin.com

HICNM0307